THE
HOUSE OF QUIET

AN AUTOBIOGRAPHY

By
Arthur Christopher Benson

PREFACE

I have been reading this morning a very pathetic and characteristic document. It is a paper that has lurked for years in an old collection of archives, a preface, sketched by a great writer, who is famous wherever the English language is spoken or read, for the second edition of a noble book. The book, on its first appearance, was savagely and cruelly attacked; and the writer of it, hurt and wounded by a mass of hateful and malevolent criticisms, piled together by an envious and narrow mind, tried, with a miserable attempt at jaunty levity, to write an answer to the vicious assailant. This answer is deeply pathetic, because, behind the desperate parade of cheerful insouciance, one seems to hear the life-blood falling, drop by drop; the life-blood of a dauntless and pure spirit, whose words had been so deftly twisted and satanically misrepresented as to seem the utterances of a sensual and cynical mind.

In deference to wise and faithful advice, the preface was withheld and suppressed; and one is thankful for that; and the episode is further|vi a tender lesson for all who have faithfully tried to express the deepest thoughts of their heart, frankly and sincerely, never to make the least attempt to answer, or apologise, or explain. If one's book, or poem, or picture survives, that is the best of all answers. If it does not survive, well, one has had one's say, thought one's thought, done one's best to enlighten, to contribute, to console; and, like millions of other human utterances, the sound is lost upon the wind, the thought, like a rainbow radiance, has shone and vanished upon the cloud.

The book which is here presented has had its share both of good and evil report; and it fell so far short of even its own simple purpose, that I should be the last to hold that it had been blamed unduly. I have no sort of intention of answering my critics; but I would wish to make plain what the book itself perhaps fails to make plain, namely, what my purpose in writing it was. The book grew rather than was made. It was, from the first, meant as a message to the weak rather than as a challenge to the strong. There is a theory of life, wielded like a cudgel by the hands of the merry and high-hearted, that the whole duty of man is to dash into the throng, to eat and drink, to|vii love and wed, to laugh and fight. That is a fine temper; it is the mood of the sailor-comrades of Odysseus—

"That ever with a frolic welcome took
The thunder and the sunshine, and opposed
Free hearts, free foreheads."

Such a mood, if it be not cruel, or tyrannous, or brutal, or overbearing, is a generous and inspiriting thing. Joined, as I have seen it joined, with simplicity and unselfishness and utter tenderness, it is the finest spirit in the world—the spirit of the great and chivalrous knight of old days. But when this mood shows itself without the kindly and gracious knightly attributes, it is a vile and ugly thing, insolent, selfish, animal.

The problem, then, which I tried to present in my book, was this: I imagined a temperament of a peaceful and gentle order, a temperament without robustness and joie de vivre, but with a sense of duty, a desire to help, an anxious wish not to shirk responsibility; and then I tried to depict such a character as being suddenly thrust into the shadow, set aside, as, by their misfortune or their fault, a very large number of persons are set aside, debarred from ambition, pushed into a backwater of life,|viii made, by some failure of vitality, into an invalid (a word which conceals many of the saddest tragedies of the world)—and I set myself to reflect how a man, with such limitations, might yet lead a life that was wholesome and contented and helpful; and then, at the last, I thought of him as confronted with a prospect of one of the deepest and sweetest blessings of life, the hope of a noble love; and then again, the tyrannous weakness that had laid him low, swept that too out of his grasp, and bade him exchange death for life, darkness for the cheerful day.

Who does not know of home after home where such things happen? of life after life, on which calamities fall, so that the best that the sufferer can do is to gather up the fragments that remain, that nothing be lost? This book, The House of Quiet, was written for all whose life, by some stroke of God, seemed dashed into fragments, and who might feel so listless, so dismayed, that they could not summon up courage even to try and save something from the desolate wreck.

To compare small things with great, it was an attempt to depict, in modern unromantic fashion, such a situation as that of Robinson|ix Crusoe, where a man is thrown suddenly upon his own resources, shut off from sympathy and hope. In that great fiction one sees the patience, the courage, the inventiveness of the simple hero grow under the author's hand; but the soul of my own poor hero had indeed suffered shipwreck, though he fell among less stimulating surroundings than the caverns and freshets, the wildfowl and the savages, of that green isle in the Caribbean Sea.

In the Life of William Morris, a man whose chosen motto was si je puis, and who, whatever else he was accused of, was never accused of a want of virile strength, there is an interesting and pathetic letter, which he wrote at the age of fifty-one, when he was being thrust, against his better judgment, into a prominent position in the Socialist movement.

"My habits are quiet and studious," he said, "and, if I am too much worried with 'politics,' i.e., intrigue, I shall be no use to the cause as a writer. All this shows, you will say, a weak man: that is true, but I must be taken as I am, not as I am not."

This sentence sums up, very courageously and faithfully, the difficulty in which many people, who believe in ideas, and perceive more[x clearly than they are able to act, are placed by honest diffidence and candid self-knowledge. We would amend life, if we could; but the impossibility lies, not in seeing what is beautiful and just and right, but in making other people desire it. It is conceivable, after all, that God knows best, and has good reasons for delay—though many men, and those not the least gallant, act as though they knew better still. But it matters very little whether we betray our own weakness, by what we say or do. What does matter is that we should have desired something ahead of us, should have pointed it out to others. We may not attain it; others may not attain it; but we have shown that we dare not acquiesce in our weakness, that we will not allow ourselves to be silent about our purer hopes, that we will not recline in a false security, that we will not try to solve the problem by overlooking its difficulties; but that we will strive to hold fast, in a tender serenity, to a belief in the strong and loving purpose of God, however dark may be the shadow that lies across the path, however sombre the mountain-barrier that lies between us and the sunlit plain.

A. C. B.

April 12, 1907.

[xi

PREFATORY NOTE TO ORIGINAL EDITION

The writer of the following pages was a distant cousin of my own, and to a certain extent a friend. That is to say, I had stayed several times with him, and he had more than once visited me at my own home. I knew that he was obliged, for reasons of health, to live a very quiet and retired life; but he was not a man who appeared to be an invalid. He was keenly interested in books, in art, and above all in people, though he had but few intimate friends. He died in the autumn of 1900, and his mother, who was his only near relation, died in the following year; it fell to me to administer his estate, and among his papers I found this book, prepared in all essential respects for publication, though it is clear that it would not have seen the light in his lifetime. I submitted it to a friend of wide literary experience; his opinion was that the book had considerable interest, and illustrated[xii a definite and peculiar point of view, besides presenting a certain attraction of style. I accordingly made arrangements for its publication; adding a few passages from the diary of the last days, which was composed subsequently to the date at which the book was arranged.

I need hardly say that the names are throughout fictitious; and I will venture to express a hope that identification will not be attempted, because the book is one which depends for its value, not on the material circumstances of the writer, but upon the views of life which he formed.

THE HOUSE OF QUIET
INTRODUCTORY
Christmas, Eve, 1898.

I have been a good deal indoors lately, and I have been amusing myself by looking through old papers and diaries of my own. It seems to me that, though the record is a very uneventful one, there is yet a certain unity throughout—I can hardly call it a conscious, definite aim, or dignify it by the name of a philosophy. But I have lived latterly with a purpose, and on a plan that has gradually shaped itself and become more coherent.

It was formerly my ambition to write a book, and it has gone the way of most ambitions. I suppose I have not the literary temperament; I have not got the instinct for form on a large scale. In the books which I have attempted to write, I have generally lost myself among details and abandoned the task in despair. I have never been capable of the fundamental brainwork; the fundamental conception which Rossetti said made all the difference between a good piece of art and a bad one. When I was young, my idea of writing was to pile fine phrases together, and to think that any topic which occurred to my mind was pertinent to the matter in hand. Now that I am older, I have learnt that form and conception are not everything but nearly everything, and that a definite idea austerely presented is better than a heap of literary ornament.

And now it seems to me that I have after all, without intending it, written a book,—the one book, that, it is said, every man has in his power to write. I feel like the King of France who said that he had "discovered" a gallery in one of his palaces by the simple process of pulling down partition walls. I have discarded a large amount of writing, but I have selected certain episodes, made extracts from my diaries, and added a few passages; and the result is the story of my life, told perhaps in a desultory way, but with a certain coherence.

Whether or no the book will ever see the light I cannot tell; probably not. I do not suppose I shall have the courage to publish it myself, and I do not know any one who is likely to take the trouble of editing it when I am gone. But there it is—the story of a simple life. Perhaps it will go the way of waste paper, kindle fires, flit in sodden dreariness about ashpits, till it is trodden in the mire. Perhaps it may repose in some dusty bookshelf, and arouse the faint and tender curiosity of some far-off inheritor of my worldly goods, like the old diaries of my forefathers which stand on my own bookshelf. But if it came to be published I think that there are some to whom it would appeal, as the thin-drawn tremor of the violin stirs the note in vase or glass that have stood voiceless and inanimate. I have borne griefs, humiliations, dark overshadowings of the spirit; there are moments when I have peered, as it were, into the dim-lit windows of hell; but I have had, too, my fragrant hours, tranquil joys, imperishable ecstasies. And as a pilgrim may tell his tale of travel to homekeeping folks, so I may allow myself the license to speak, and tell what of good and evil the world has brought me, and of my faint strivings after that interior peace, which can be found, possessed, and enjoyed.

1
Dec. 7, 1897.

My Room
I sit this evening, towards the end of the year, in a deep arm-chair in a large, low panelled room that serves me as bedroom and study together: the windows are hung with faded tapestry curtains; there is a great open tiled fireplace before me, with logs red-crumbling, bedded in grey ash, every now and then winking out flame and lighting up the lean iron dogs that support the fuel; odd Dutch tiles pave and wall the cavernous hearth—this one a quaint galleon in full sail on a viscous, crested sea; that, a stout sleek bird standing in complacent tranquillity; at the back of the hearth, with the swift shadows flickering over it, is a large iron panel showing a king in a war chariot, with a flying cloak, issuing from an arched portal, upon a bridge which spans a furious stream, and shaking out the reins of two stamping steeds; on the high chimney-board is a row of Delft plates. The room is furnished with no precision or propriety, the furniture having drifted in fortuitously as it was needed: here is a tapestried couch; there an oak bookcase crammed with a strange assortment of books; here a tall press; a

picture or two—a bishop embedded in lawn with a cauliflower wig; a crayon sketch of a scholarly head. There is no plan of decoration—all fantastic miscellany. At the far end, under an arch of oak, stands a bed, screened from the room by a dark leather screen. Outside, all is unutterably still, not with the stillness that sometimes falls on a sleeping town, where the hush seems invaded by imperceptible cries, but with the deep tranquillity of the countryside nestling down into itself. The trees are silent. Listening intently, I can hear the trickle of the mill-leat, and the murmur of the hazel-hidden stream; but that slumbrous sound ministers, as it were, the dreamful quality, like the breathing of the sleeper—enough, and not more than enough, to give the sense of sleeping life, as opposed to the aching, icy stillness of death.

2
Early Days
I may speak shortly of my parentage and circumstances. I was the only son of my father, a man who held a high administrative position under Government. He owed his advancement not to family connections, for our family though ancient was obscure. No doubt it may be urged that all families are equally ancient, but what I mean is that our family had for many generations preserved a sedulous tradition of gentle blood through poverty and simple service. My ancestors had been mostly clergymen, doctors, lawyers—at no time had we risen to the dignity of a landed position or accumulated wealth: but we had portraits, miniatures, plate—in no profusion, but enough to be able to feel that for a century or two we had enjoyed a liberal education, and had had opportunities for refinement if not leisure, and aptitude for cultivating the arts of life; it had not been a mere sordid struggle, an inability to escape from the coarsening pressure of gross anxieties, but something gracious, self-contained, benevolent, active.

My father changed this; his profession brought him into contact with men of rank and influence; he was fitted by nature to play a high social part; he had an irresistible geniality, and something of a courtly air. He married late, the daughter of an impoverished offshoot of a great English family, and I was their only child.

The London life is dim to me; I faintly recollect being brought into the room in a velvet suit to make my bow to some assembled circle of guests. I remember hearing from the nursery the din and hubbub of a dinner-party rising, in faint gusts, as the door was opened and shut—even of brilliant cascades of music sparkling through the house when I awoke after a first sleep, in what seemed to me some dead hour of the night. But my father had no wish to make me into a precocious monkey, playing self-conscious tricks for the amusement of visitors, and I lived for the most part in the company of my mother—herself almost a child—and my faithful nurse, a small, simple-minded Yorkshire woman, who had been my mother's nurse before.

When I was about six years old my father died suddenly, and the first great shock of my life was the sight of the handsome waxen face, with the blurred and flinty look of the dulled eyes, the leaden pallor of the thin hands crossed on his breast; to this day I can see the blue shadows of the ruffled shroud about his neck and wrists.

Our movements were simple enough. Only that summer, owing to an accession of wealth, my father and mother had determined on some country home to which they might retire in his months of freedom. My mother had never cared for London; together they had found in the heart of the country a house that attracted both of them, and a long lease had been taken within a week or two of my father's death. Our furniture was at once transferred thither, and from that hour it has been my home.

3
The Home Land
The region in which I live is a land of ridge and vale, as though it had been ploughed with a gigantic plough. The high-roads lie as a rule along the backs of the uplands, and the villages stand on the windy heights. The lines of railway which run along the valley tend to create a new species of valley village, but the old hamlets, with their grey-stone high-backed churches, with slender shingled spires, stand aloft, the pure air racing over them. The ancient manors and granges are as a rule built in the more sheltered and sequestered valleys, approached from the high-road by winding wood-lanes of exquisite beauty. The soil is sandy, and a soft stone is quarried in many places by the road-side, leaving quaint miniature cliffs and bluffs of weathered yellow, sometimes so evenly stratified as to look like a rock-temple or a buried ruin with mouldering buttresses; about these pits grow little knots of hazels and ash-suckers, and the whole is hung in summer with luxuriant creepers and climbing plants, out of which the crumbling rock-surfaces emerge. The roads go down very steeply to the valleys, which are thick-set with copse and woodland, and at the bottom runs a full-fed stream, with cascades and pebbly shingles, running dark under scarps of sandstone, or hidden deep under thick coverts of hazel, the water in the light a pure

grey-green. Some chalk is mingled with these ridges, so that in rainy weather the hoof-prints in the roads ooze as with milk. The view from these uplands is of exquisite beauty, ridge after ridge rolling its soft outlines, thinly wooded. Far away are glimpses of high heathery tracts black with pines, or a solitary clump upon some naked down. But the views in the valleys are even more beautiful. The steep wood rises from the stream, or the grave lines of some tilted fallow; in summer the water-plants grow with rich luxuriance by the rivulet, tall willow-herb and velvety loosestrife, tufted meadowsweet, and luxuriant comfrey. The homesteads are of singular stateliness, with their great brick chimney-stacks, the upper storeys weather-tiled and the roof of flat tiles of sandstone; the whole mellowed by orange and grey lichens till the houses seem to have sprung from the very soil.

4
Golden End

My own home—bearing the tranquil name of Golden End—is an ancient manor; out of a sandy lane turns an avenue of great Scotch firs, passing the house and inclining gradually in its direction. The house is a strange medley; one part of it is an Elizabethan building, mullioned, of grey stone; one wing is weather-tiled and of simple outline. The front, added at some period of prosperity, is Georgian, thickly set with large windows; over all is a little tiled cupola where an alarm bell hangs. There is a small square garden in front surrounded by low walls; above the house lies what was once a bowling-green, with a terraced walk surrounding it. The kitchen garden comes close up to the windows, and is protected on the one side by a gigantic yew hedge, like a green bastion, on the other by an ancient stone wall, with a tiled roof; below the house lie quaint farm-buildings, cartsheds, barns, granaries, and stables; beyond them are pools, fringed with self-sown ashes, and an orchard, in the middle of which stands a brick dovecot with sandstone tiles. The meadows fall from the house to the stream; but the greater part of the few acres which we hold is simple woodland, where the copse grows thick and dark, with here and there a stately forest tree. The house seen, as I love best to see it, from the avenue on a winter evening, rises a dark irregular pile, crowned with the cupola and the massive chimneys against a green and liquid sky, in which trembles a single star; the pine-trees are blacker still; and below lies the dim mysterious woodland, with the mist rising over the stream, and, beyond that, soft upland after upland, like a land of dreams, out to the horizon's verge.

Within all is dark and low; there is a central panelled hall with round oak arches on either hand leading through little anterooms to a parlour and dining-room. There are wide, meaningless corridors with steps up and down that connect the wings with the central building; the staircases are of the most solid oak. All the rooms are panelled except the attics, which show the beams crossing in the ancient plasterwork. At the top of the house is a long room which runs from end to end, with a great open fireplace. The kitchen is a huge, paved chamber with an oak pillar in the centre. A certain amount of massive oak furniture, sideboards, chests, and presses, with initials or dates, belongs to the place; but my father was a great collector of books, china, and pictures, which, with the furniture of a large London house, were put hurriedly in, with little attempt at order; and no one has since troubled to arrange them. One little feature must be mentioned; at the top of the house a crazy oak door gives access to a flight of stairs that leads on to a parapet; but below the stairs is a tiny oratory, with an altar and some seats, where the household assemble every morning for a few prayers, and together sing an artless hymn.

5
My Mother

My mother, who through the following pages must be understood to be the presiding deity of the scene—O quam te memorem?—how shall I describe her? Seen through her son's eyes she has an extraordinary tranquillity and graciousness of mien. She moves slowly with an absolutely unconscious dignity. She is naturally very silent, and has a fixed belief that she is entirely devoid of all intellectual power, which is in one sense true, for she reads little and has no taste for discussion. At the same time she is gifted with an extraordinary shrewdness and penetration in practical matters, and I would trust her judgment without hesitation. She is intensely affectionate, and has the largest heart I have ever known; but at the same time is capable of taking almost whimsical prejudices against people, which, however I have combated them at the time, have generally proved to be justified by subsequent events. Her sympathy and her geniality make her delightful company, for she delights in listening to the talk of clever people and has a strong sense of humour. She likes being read to, though I do not think she questions the thought of what is read. She is deeply religious, though I do not suppose she could give a reason for her faith, and is constantly tolerant of religious differences which she never attempts to comprehend. In the village she is simply adored by men, women, and children alike, though she is not particularly given to what is called "visiting the poor."

At the same time if there is trouble in any house, no matter of what kind, she goes there straight by instinct, and has none of the dread of emotional scenes which make so many of us cowards in the presence of sorrow and suffering. I do not think she feels any duty about it, but it is as natural and spontaneous for her to go as it is for most of us to desire to keep away. A shrewd woman of the village, a labourer's wife, whom my mother had seen through a dreadful tragedy a year or two before, once said in reply to a question of mine, "It isn't as if her ladyship said or did more than any one else—every one was kind to us—but she used to come in and sit with me and look at me, and after a little I used to feel that it was all right."

She manages the household with less expenditure of trouble than I have ever seen. Our servants never seem to leave us; they are paid what many people would call absurdly high wages, but I do not think that is the attraction. My mother does not see very much of them, and finds fault, when rarely necessary, with a simple directness which I have in vain tried to emulate; but her displeasure is so impersonal that there seems to be no sting in it. It is not that they have failed in their duty to herself, but they have been untrue to the larger duty to which she is herself obedient.

She never seems to labour under any strong sense of the imperative duty of philanthropic activity—indeed it is hard to say how her days are filled—but in her simplicity, her unselfishness, her quiet acceptance of the conditions of life, her tranquillity and her devoted lovingness she seems to me the best Christian I have ever seen, and to come nearest to the ideals of Christ. But, though a large part of her large income is spent in unostentatious benevolence, she would think it preposterous if it were suggested to her that Christianity demanded an absolute sacrifice of worldly possessions. Yet she sets no store on comfort or the evidences of wealth; she simply accepts them, and has a strong instinctive feeling of stewardship.

I cannot help thinking that such women are becoming rarer; and yet it is hard to believe that they can ever have been other than rare.

6

I gratefully acknowledge the constant presence of an element in my life which for want of a better name I will call the sense of beauty. I mean by that the unaccountable thrill of emotion by which one is sometimes surprised, often quite suddenly and unexpectedly; this sense of wonder, which darts upon the mind with an almost physical sensation, seems to come in two different ways. With some, the majority I believe, it originates entirely in personal relations with other human beings and is known as love; with others it arises over a larger region, and is inspired by a sudden perception of some incommunicable beauty in a flower, a scent, a view, a picture, a poem. Those in whom the latter sense predominates are, I think, less apt to be affected by human relationships, but pass through the world in a certain solitary and wistful mood, with perhaps more wide and general sources of happiness but less liable to be stirred to the depths of their being by a friendship or a passion. To take typical examples of such a class I conceive that Wordsworth and William Morris were instances. Wordsworth derived, I believe, his highest inspiration from the solemn dignities of nature, in her most stupendous and majestic forms; while to Morris belonged that power, which amounted in him to positive genius, for seeing beauty in the most homely and simple things.

Beauty and Mystery

I was myself haunted from a very early date by the sense of beauty and mystery, though not for many years could I give it a name; but I have found in my case that it originated as a rule in some minute effect of natural things. I have seen some of the wildest and most astounding natural prospects in Europe; I have climbed high rocky peaks and threaded mountain solitudes, but some overshadowing of horror and awe has robbed emotion of its most intimate joy; and I have always found myself more thrilled by some tranquil vignette—the moon rising through a forest glade, a red sunset between the boughs of pines, the crisping wave of some broken eddy, the "green-dense and dim-delicious" depth of a woodland pool, the weathered gables of an ancient manor, an orchard white with the snows of spring—than I have ever been by the sight of the most solemn mountain-head or the furious breakers of some uncontrolled tide.

Two or three of these sacred sights I may venture to describe, taking them at random out of the treasure-house of memory; two belong to my schooldays. I was a pupil at a big suburban school; the house which we inhabited had once been the villa of a well-known statesman, and had large and dignified grounds, where with certain restrictions, we were allowed to ramble. They were bounded on one side by a high paling, inaccessible to small limbs, and a vague speculation as to what was behind the fence long dwelt with me. One day, however, I found that I could loose a portion of a broken paling, and looking through I saw a quiet place, the tail of a neglected shrubbery; the spot seemed quite unvisited; the laurels grew thickly about, and tall elms gave an austere gloom to the little glade; the ground was pathless, and thickly overgrown with periwinkles, but in the centre were three tiny grave-mounds, the graves, I have since reflected, of dogs, but which I at the time supposed to be the graves of children. I gazed with a singular sense of mystery, and strange dream-pictures rose instinctively in my mind, weaving themselves over the solitary and romantic spot. It is strange how often in dreams and gentle reveries I have visited the place.

The Enchanted Land
The next is a later vision. Near the public school where I was educated lay a forest to which we had free admittance. I found that by hard walking it was just possible to reach a wooded hill which was a conspicuous feature of the distant landscape, but the time at my disposal between two school engagements never sufficed to penetrate farther. From the top of this hill it was possible to get a view of a large tract of forest ground, an open grassy glade, with large trees of towering greenness standing sentinel on either side; the bracken grew luxuriantly in places, and at the end of the glade was a glint of water in the horn of some forest pool. This place was to me a veritable "magic casement"; beyond lay the enchanted land into which I could not penetrate, the blue hills on the horizon seen over the tree-tops. I never dreamt of them as inhabited by human beings like myself, but as some airy region, with leagues of dreaming woods and silent forest spaces. At times a deer would slowly cross the open vale, and stand to sniff the breeze; the very cooing of the doves in their leafy fastnesses had a richer and drowsier sound.

But the home of incommunicable dreams, beyond all others, is to me a certain mill—Grately Mill—that is not many miles from my present home. My mother had an old aunt who lived in a pleasant house in the neighbourhood, and we used to go there when I was a child to spend a few weeks of the early summer.

A little vague lane led to it: a lane that came from nowhere in particular, and took you nowhere; meandering humbly among the pastures wherever it was convenient to them to permit it, like a fainthearted Christian. Hard by was a tall, high-shouldered, gabled farm of red brick, with a bell perched on the roof in a white pavilion of its own. Down the lane on hot summer days we used to walk—my mother and I: my mother whom I revered as a person of unapproachable age and dim experience, though she had been in the schoolroom herself but a year or two before my birth; I trotting by her side with a little fishing-rod in a grey holland case, to fish for perch in the old pond at the Hall.

The lane grew sandier and damper: a rivulet clucked in the ditch, half-hidden in ragged-robin with its tattered finery, and bright varnished ranunculus; the rivulet was a mysterious place enough ever since the day when we found it full of waving clusters of strange dark creatures, more eel than fish, which had all appeared with miraculous unanimity in a single night—lamperns, the village naturalist called them, and told us that in ancient days they were a delicacy; while I, in my childish mind, at once knew that it was this which had gone to the composition of that inexplicable dish, a surfeit of lampreys, as the history had it, of which some greedy monarch died.

Once, too, a bright-coloured eel had been seen at a certain point, who had only just eluded the grasp of hot little fingers. How many times I looked for master eel, expecting to meet him at the same place, and was careful to carry a delightful tin box in my pocket, in which he might travel home in my pocket, and live an honoured life in a basin in the night nursery. Poor eel! I am glad now that he escaped, but then he was only a great opportunity missed—an irreparable regret.

Grately Mill
Then the poor lane, which had been getting more like a water-course every moment, no longer made any pretence, and disappeared into a shallow sheet of clear water—the mill at last! The scene, as I remember it, had a magical charm. On the left, by the side of the lane, rose a crazy footpath of boards and posts with a wooden handrail, and a sluice or two below. Beyond, the deep mill-pool slept, dark and still, all fringed with trees. On the right the stream flowed off among the meadows, disappearing into an arch of greenery; in summer the banks and islets were all overgrown with tall rich plants, comfrey, figwort, water-dock. The graceful willow-herb hung its pink horns; the loosestrife rose in sturdier velvet spires. On the bank stood the shuttered, humming mill, the water-wheel splashing and thundering, like a prisoned giant, in a penthouse of its own. It was a fearful joy to look in and see it rise dripping, huge and black, with the fresh smell of the river water all about it. All the mill was powdered with the dust of grain; the air inside was full of floating specks; the hoppers rattled, and the gear grumbled in the roof, while the flour streamed merrily into the open sack. The miller, a grave preoccupied man, all dusted over, like a plum, with a thin bloom of flour, gave us a grave nod of greeting, which seemed to make us free of the place. I dare say he was a shy mild man, with but little of the small change of the mind at his disposal; but he seemed to me then an austere and statesmanlike person, full to the brim of grave affairs. Beyond the mill, a lane of a more determined character led through arches of elms to the common. And now, on secular days, the interests of the chase took precedence of all else; but there were Sundays in the summer when we walked to attend Grately Church. It seems to me at this lapse of time to have been almost impossibly antique. Ancient yews stood by it, and it had a white boarded spire with a cracked bell. Inside, the single aisleless nave, with ancient oak pews, was much encumbered in one place by a huge hand-organ, with a forest of gold pipes, turned by a wizened man, who opened a little door in the side and

inserted his hand at intervals to set the tune. The clergyman, an aged gentleman, wore what was, I suppose, a dark wig, though at the time I imagined it to be merely an agreeable variety on ordinary hair; another pleasant habit he had of slightly smacking his lips, at every little pause, as he read, which gave an air of indescribable gusto to the service:—"Moab—tut—is my washpot—tut—; over Edom—tut—will I cast out my shoe—tut—; upon Philistia—tut—will I triumph."

Grately Church
In the vestry of the church reposed a curious relic—a pyx, I believe, is the correct name. It was a gilded metal chalice with a top, into which, if my memory serves me, were screwed little soldiers to guard the sacred body; these were loose, and how I coveted them! In the case were certain spikes and branches of crystal, the broken remains, I believe, of a spreading crystal tree which once adorned the top. How far my memory serves me I know not, but I am sure that the relic which may still survive, is a most interesting thing; and I can recollect that when a high dignitary of the Church stayed with us, it was kindly brought over by the clergyman for his inspection, and his surprise was very great.

The Hall lay back from the common, sheltered by great trees. The house itself, a low white building, was on those summer days cool and fragrant. The feature of the place was the great fish-ponds—one lay outside the shrubbery; but another, formerly I believe a monastic stew-pond, was a long rectangle just outside the windows of the drawing-room, and only separated from it by a gravel walk: along part of it ran an ancient red-brick wall. This was our favourite fishing-place; but above it, brooded over by huge chestnuts, lay a deeper and stiller pond, half covered with water-lilies—too sacred and awful a place to be fished in or even visited alone.

Upon the fishing hours I do not love to dwell; I would only say that of such cruelties as attended it I was entirely innocent. I am sure that I never thought of a perch as other than a delightful mechanical thing, who had no grave objection to being hauled up gasping, with his black stripes gleaming, and prickling his red fins, to be presently despatched, and carried home stiff and cold in a little basket.

The tea under the tall trees of the lawn; the admiring inspection of our prey; the stuffed dog in the hall with his foot upon a cricket-ball—all these are part of the dream-pictures; and the whole is invested for me with the purpureal gleams of childhood.

Grately Thirty Years After

The other day I found myself on a bicycle near enough to Grately to make it possible to go there; into the Hall grounds I did not venture, but I struck across the common and went down the lane to the mill. I was almost ashamed of the agitation I felt, but the sight of the common, never visited for nearly thirty years, induced a singular physical distress. It was not that everything had grown smaller, even changed the places that they occupy in my mental picture, but a sort of homesickness seemed to draw tight bands across my heart. What does it mean, this intense local attachment, for us flimsy creatures, snapped at a touch, and with so brief a pilgrimage? A strange thought! The very intensity and depth of the feeling seems to confer on it a right to permanence.

The lane came abruptly to an end by the side of a commonplace, straight-banked, country brook. There were no trees, no water-plants; the road did not dip to the stream, and in front of me lay a yellow brick bridge, with grim iron lattices. Alas! I had mistaken the turn, and must retrace my steps. But stay! what was that squat white house by the waterside? It was indeed the old mill, with its boarded projections swept away, its barns gone, its garden walled with a neat wall. The old high-timbered bridge was down; some generous landlord had gone to great expense, and Grately had a good convenient road, a sensible bridge, and an up-to-date mill. Probably there was not a single person in the parish who did not confess to an improvement.

But who will give me back the tall trees and the silent pool? Who will restore the ancient charm, the delicate mysteries, the gracious dignity of the place? Is beauty a mere trick of grouping, the irradiation of a golden mood, a chance congeries of water and high trees and sunlight? If beauty be industriously hunted from one place by ruthless hands, does she spread her wings and fly? Is the restless, ceaseless effort of nature to restore beauty to the dismal messes made by man, simply broken off and made vain? Or has she leisure to work harder yet in unvisited places, patiently enduring the grasp of the spoiling hand?

It was with something like a sob that I turned away. But of one thing no one can rob me, and that is the picture of Grately Mill, glorified indeed by the patient worship of years, which is locked into some portfolio of the mind, and can be unspread in a moment before the gazing eye.

Egeria
And for one thing I can be grateful—that the still spirit of sweet and secret places, that wayward nymph who comes and goes, with the wind in her hair and the gleam of deep water in her eyes—she to whom we give

many a clumsy name—that she first beckoned to me and spoke words in my ear beneath the high elms of Grately Mill. Many times have we met and spoken in secret since, my Egeria and I; many times has she touched my shoulder, and whispered a magic charm. That presence has been often withdrawn from me; but I have but to recall the bridge, the water-plants, the humming mill, the sunlight on the sandy shallows, to feel her hand in mine again.

7

As a boy and a young man I went through the ordinary classical education—private school, public school, and university. I do not think I troubled my head at the time about the philosophical theory or motive of the course; but now, looking back upon it after an interval of twenty years, while my admiration of the theory of it is enhanced, as a lofty and dignified scheme of mental education, I find myself haunted by uneasy doubts as to its practical efficacy. While it seems to me to be for a capable and well-equipped boy with decided literary taste, a noble and refining influence, I begin to fear that for the large majority of youthful English minds it is narrowing, unimproving, and conspicuous for an absence of intellectual enjoyment.

Is it not the experience of most people that little boys are conscientious, duty-loving, interested not so much in the matter of work, but in the zealous performance of it; and that when adolescence begins, they grow indifferent, wearied, even rebellious, until they drift at last into a kind of cynicism about the whole thing—a kind of dumb certainty, that whatever else may be got from work, enjoyment in no form is the result? And is not the moral of this, that the apprenticeship once over and the foundation laid, special tastes should as far as possible be consulted, and subjects simplified, so as to give boys a sense of mastery in something, and interest at all hazards.

Methods of Study
The champions of our classical system defend it on the ground that the accurate training in the subtleties of grammar hardens and fortifies the intelligence, and that the mind is introduced to the masterpieces of ancient literature, and thus encouraged in the formation of correct taste and critical appreciation.

An excellent theory, and I admit at once its value for minds of high and firm intellectual calibre. But how does it actually work out for the majority?

In the first place, look at what the study of grammar amounts to—it comes, as a matter of fact, when one remembers the grammar papers which were set in examinations, to be little more than a knowledge of arbitrary, odd and eccentric forms such as a boy seldom if ever meets in the course of his reading. Imagine teaching English on the same theory, and making boys learn that metals have no plural, or that certain fish use the same form in the singular and in the plural—things of which one acquires the knowledge insensibly, and which are absolutely immaterial. Moreover, the quantity of grammatical forms in Latin and Greek are infinitely increased by the immensely larger number of inflexions. Is it useful that boys should have to commit to memory the dual forms in Greek verbs—forms of a repulsive character in themselves, and seldom encountered in books? The result of this method is that the weaker mind is warped and strained. Some few memories of a peculiarly retentive type may acquire these useless facts in a mechanical manner; but it is hardly more valuable than if they were required to commit to memory long lists of nonsense words. Yet in most cases they are doomed to be speedily and completely forgotten—indeed, nothing can ever be really learnt unless a logical connection can be established between the items.

Mastery and Spirit
Then after the dark apprenticeship of grammar comes the next stage—the appreciation of literature; but I diffidently believe here that not ten per cent of the boys who are introduced to the classics have ever the slightest idea that they are in the presence of literature at all. They never approach the point which is essential to a love of literature—the instinctive perception of the intrinsic beauty of majestic and noble words, and still less the splendid associations which grow to be inseparably connected with words, in a language which one really knows and admires.

Method and Spirit
My own belief is that both the method of instruction and the spirit of that instruction are at fault. Like the Presbyterian Liturgy, the system depends far too much on the individuality of the teacher, and throws too great a strain upon his mood. A vigorous, brilliant, lively, humorous, rhetorical man can break through the shackles of construing and parsing, and give the boys the feeling of having been in contact with a larger mind; but in the hands of a dull and uninspiring teacher the system is simply famishing from its portentous aridity. The result, at all events, is that the majority of the boys at our schools never get the idea that they are in the presence of literature at all. They are kept kicking their heels in the dark and

cold antechamber of parsing and grammar, and never get a glimpse of the bright gardens within.

What is, after all, the aim of education? I suppose it is twofold: firstly, to make of the mind a bright, keen, and effective instrument, capable of seeing a point, of grappling with a difficulty, of presenting facts or thoughts with clearness and precision. A young man properly educated should be able to detect a fallacy, to correct by acquired clearsightedness a false logical position. He should not be at the mercy of any new theory which may be presented to him in a specious and attractive shape. That is, I suppose, the negative side. Then secondly, he should have a cultivated taste for intellectual things, a power of enjoyment; he should not bow meekly to authority in the matter of literature, and force himself into the admiration of what is prescribed, but he should be possessed of a dignified and wholesome originality; he should have his own taste clearly defined. If his bent is historical, he should be eagerly interested in any masterly presentation of historical theory, whether new or old; if philosophical, he should keep abreast of modern speculation; if purely literary, he should be able to return hour after hour to masterpieces that breathe and burn.

Educational Results
But what is the result of our English education? In one respect admirable; it turns out boys who are courteous, generous, brave, active, and public-spirited; but is it impossible that these qualities should exist with a certain intellectual standard? I remember now, though I did not apply any theory at the time to the phenomenon, that when at school I used dimly to wonder at seeing boys who were all these things—fond of talk, fond of games, devoted to all open-air exercises, conscientious and wholesome-minded, who were at the same time utterly listless in intellectual things—who could not read a book of any kind except the simplest novel, and then only to fill a vacant hour, who could not give a moment's attention to the presentment of an interesting episode, who were moreover utterly contemptuous of all such things, inclined to think them intolerably tedious and essentially priggish—and yet these were the boys of whom most was made, who were most popular not only with boys but with masters as well, and who, in our little microcosmography were essentially the successful people, to be imitated, followed, and worshipped.

Now if it were certain that the qualities which are developed by an English education would be sacrificed if a higher intellectual standard were aimed at, I should not hesitate to sacrifice the intellectual side. But I do not believe it is necessary; and what is stranger still, I do not believe that most of our educators have any idea that the intellectual side of education is being sacrificed.

I remember once hearing a veteran and successful educator say that he considered a well-educated man was a man whose mind was not at the mercy of the last new book on any ordinary subject. If that is an infallible test, then our public schools may be said to have succeeded beyond all reasonable expectation. The ordinary public-school type of man is not in the least at the mercy of the last new book, because he is careful never to submit himself to the chance of pernicious bias—he does not get so far as to read it.

Educational Aims
At present athletics are so much deferred to, that boys seem to me to be encouraged deliberately to lay their plans as if life ended at thirty. But I believe that schools should aim at producing a type that should develop naturally and equably with the years. What we want to produce is an unselfish, tranquil, contented type, full of generous visions; neither prematurely serious nor incurably frivolous, nor afraid of responsibility, nor morbidly desirous of influence; neither shunning nor courting publicity, but natural, wholesome, truthful, and happy; not afraid of difficulties nor sadly oppressed with a sense of responsibility; fond of activity and yet capable of using and enjoying leisure; not narrow-minded, not viewing everything from the standpoint of a particular town or parish, but patriotic and yet not insular, modern-spirited and yet not despising the past, practical and yet with a sense of spiritual realities.

I think that what is saddest is that the theoretical perfection screens the practical inutility of the thing. If it seems good to the collective wisdom of the country to let education go, and to make a public-school a kind of healthy barrack-life for the physical training of the body, with a certain amount of mental occupation to fill the vacant hours that might otherwise be mischievous—pleasure with a hem of duty—let it be frankly admitted that it is so; but that the education received by boys at our public-schools is now, except in intention, literary—that is the position which I entirely deny.

Personally I had a certain feeble taste for literature. I read in a slipshod way a good deal of English poetry, memoirs, literary history, and essays, but my reading was utterly amateurish and unguided. I even had some slight preferences in style, but I could not have given a reason for my preference; I could not write an English essay—I had no idea of arrangement. I had never been told to "let the bones show;" I had no sense of proportion, and considered that anything which I happened to have in my own mind was relevant to any subject about which I was writing. I had never learnt to see the point or to insist upon the essential.

The Classics

Neither do I think that I can claim to have had any particular love for the classics; but I was blest with a pictorial mind, and though much of my classical reading was a mere weariness to me, I was cheered at intervals by a sudden romantic glimpse of some scene or other that seized me with a vivid reality. The Odyssey and the Æneid were rich in these surprises; for the talk of Gods, indeed, I had nothing but bewildered contempt; but such a scene as that of Laertes in his patched gaiters, fumbling with a young tree on his upland farm, at once seized tyrannically upon my fancy. Catullus, Horace, even Martial, gave me occasional food for the imagination; and all at once it seemed worth while to traverse the arid leagues, or to wade, as Tennyson said, in a sea of glue, for these divine moments.

One such scene that affected my fancy I will describe in greater detail; and let it stand as a specimen. It was in the third Æneid; we were sitting in a dusty class-room, the gas flaring. The lesson proceeded slowly and wearily, with a thin trickle of exposition from the desk, emanating from a master who was evidently as sick of the whole business as ourselves.

Andromache, widow of Hector, after a forced union with Neoptolemus, becomes the bride of Helenus, Hector's brother. Helenus on the death of Pyrrhus becomes his successor in the chieftainship, and Andromache is once more a queen. She builds a rustic altar, an excuse for lamentation, and there bewails the memory of her first lord. I was reflecting that she must have made but a dreary wife for Helenus, when in a moment the scene was changed. Æneas, it will be remembered, comes on her in her orisons, with his troop of warriors behind him, and is greeted by the terrified queen, who believes him to be an apparition, with a wild and artless question ending a burst of passionate grief: "If you come from the world of spirits," she says, "Hector ubi est?" It is one of those sudden turns that show the ineffable genius of Virgil.

I saw in a moment a clearing in a wood of beeches; one great tree stood out from the rest. Half hidden in the foliage stood a tall stone pillar, supporting a mouldering urn. Close beside this was a stone alcove, with a little altar beneath it. In the alcove stood a silent listening statue with downcast head. From the altar went up a little smoke; the queen herself, a slender figure, clad in black, with pale worn face and fragile hands, bent in prayer. By her side were two maidens, also in the deepest black, a priest in stiff vestments, and a boy bearing a box of incense.

Virgil

A slight noise falls on the ear of Andromache; she turns, and there at the edge of a green forest path, lit by the red light of a low smouldering sun, stands the figure of a warrior, his arms rusty and dark, his mailed feet sunk in the turf, leaning on his spear. His face is pale and heavily lined, worn with ungentle experience, and lit by a strange light of recognition. His pale forked beard falls on his breast; behind him a mist of spears.

This was the scene; very rococo, no doubt, and romantic, but so intensely real, so glowing, that I could see the pale-stemmed beeches; and below, through a gap, low fantastic hills and a wan river winding in the plain. I could see the white set face of Æneas, the dark-eyed glance of the queen, the frightened silence of the worshippers.

8

At Cambridge things were not very different. I was starved intellectually by the meagre academical system. I took up the Classical Tripos, and read, with translations, in the loosest style imaginable, great masses of classical literature, caring little about the subject matter, seldom reading the notes, with no knowledge of history, archæology, or philosophy, and even strangely ignorant of idiom. I received no guidance in these matters; my attendance at lectures was not insisted upon; and the composition lecturers, though conscientious, were not inspiring men. My tutor did, it must be confessed, make some attempt to influence my reading, urging me to lay down a regular plan, and even recommending books and editions. But I was too dilatory to carry it out; and though I find that in one Long Vacation I read through the Odyssey, the Æneid, and the whole of Aristotle's Ethics, yet they left little or no impression on my mind. I did indeed drift into a First Class, but this was merely due to familiarity with, rather than knowledge of, the Classics; and my ignorance of the commonest classical rules was phenomenal.

Cambridge Life

But I did derive immense intellectual stimulus from my Cambridge life, though little from the prescribed course of study; for I belonged to a little society that met weekly, and read papers on literary and ethical subjects, prolonging a serious, if fitful, discussion late into the night. I read a great deal of English in a sketchy way, and even wrote both poetry and fiction; but I left Cambridge a thoroughly uneducated man, without an idea of literary method, and contemning accuracy and precision in favour of brilliant and heady writing. The initial impulse to interest in literature was certainly instinctive in me; but I maintain that not only did that interest never receive encouragement from the professed educators under whose influence I passed, but that I was not even professionally trained in the matter; that solidity and accuracy were never insisted upon; and that the definiteness, which at least education is capable of communicating, was either never imparted by mental processes, or that I successfully resisted the imparting of it—indeed, never knew that any attempt was being made to teach me the value or necessity of it.

9

I had a religious bringing-up. I was made familiar with the Bible and the offices of religion; only the natural piety was wanting. I am quite certain I had no sense of religion as a child—I do not think I had any morality. Like many children, I was ruled by associations rather than by principles. I was sensitive to disapproval; and being timid by nature, I was averse to being found out; being moreover lacking in vitality, I seldom experienced the sensation of being brought face to face with temptation—rebellion, anger, and sensual impulse were unknown to me; but while I was innocent, I was unconscientious and deceitful, not so much deliberately as instinctively.

The sense of religion I take to be, in its simplest definition, the consciousness of the presence of the Divine Being, and the practice of religion to be the maintenance of conscious union or communion with the Divine. These were entirely lacking to me. I accepted the fact of God's existence as I accepted the facts of history and geography. But my conception of God, if I may speak plainly and without profanity, was derived from the Old Testament, and was destitute of attractiveness. I conceived of Him as old, vindictive, unmerciful, occupied in tedious matters, hostile to all gaiety and juvenility; totally uninterested in the human race, except in so far that He regarded their transgressions with morbid asperity and a kind of gloomy satisfaction, as giving Him an opportunity of exercising coercive discipline. He was never represented to me as the Giver of the simple joys of life—of light and warmth, of food and sleep, as the Creator of curious and sweet-smelling flowers, of aromatic shrubs, of waving trees, of horned animals and extravagant insects. Considering how entirely creatures of sense children are, it has seemed to me since that it would be well if their simplest pleasures, the material surroundings of their lives, were connected with the idea of God—if they felt that what they enjoyed was sent by Him; if it were said of a toy that "God sends you this;"

or of some domestic festivity that "God hopes that you will be happy to-day,"—it appears to me that we should have less of that dreary philosophy which connects "God's will" only with moments of bereavement and suffering. If we could only feel with Job, that God, who sends us so much that is sweet and wholesome, has equally the right to send us what is evil, we could early grow to recognise that, when the greater part of our lives is made up of what is desirable or interesting, and when we cling to life and the hope of happiness with so unerring an instinct, it is probable, nay, certain, that our afflictions must be ultimately intended to minister to the fulness of joy.

Religion
Certainly religious practices, though I enjoyed them in many ways, had no effect on conduct; indeed, I never thought of them as having any concern with conduct. Religious services never seemed to me in childhood to be solemnities designed for the hallowing of life, or indeed as having any power to do so, but merely as part of the framework of duty, as ceremonies out of which it was possible to derive a certain amount of interest and satisfaction.

Church was always a pleasure to me; I liked the mise-en-scène, the timbered roof, the fallen day, the stained glass, the stone pillars, the comfortable pew, the rubricated prayer-book, the music, the movements of the minister—these all had a definite æsthetic effect upon me; moreover, it was a pleasure to note, with the unshrinking gaze of childhood, the various delightful peculiarities of members of the congregation: the old man with apple-red cheeks, in his smock-frock, who came with rigid, creaking boots to his place; the sexton, with his goat-like beard; the solicitor, who emitted sounds in the hymns like the lowing of a cow; the throaty tenor, who had but one vowel for all; the dowager in purple silk, who sat through the Psalms and inspected her prayer-book through a gold eye-glass as though she were examining some natural curiosity. All these were, in childish parlance, "so funny." And Church was thus a place to which I went willingly and joyfully; the activity of my observation saved me from the tedium with which so many children regard it.

Religious Sentiment
This vacuous æstheticism in the region of religion continued with me through my school days. Of purpose and principle there was no trace. I do indeed remember one matter in which I had recourse to prayer. At my private school, a big suburban establishment, I was thrust into a large dormitory, a shrinking and bewildered atom, fresh from the privacies and loving attentions of the nursery, and required to undress and go to bed before the eyes of fifty boys. It was a rude introduction to the world, and it

is strange to reflect upon the helpless despair with which a little soul can be filled under circumstances which to maturer thoughts appear almost idyllic. But while I crouched miserably upon my bed, as I prepared to slip between the sheets—of which the hard texture alone dismayed me—I was struck by a shoe, mischievously, but not brutally thrown by a bigger boy some yards away. Is it amusing or pathetic to reflect that night after night I prayed that this might not be repeated, using a suffrage of the Litany about our persecutors and slanderers, which seemed to me dismally appropriate?

At the public school to which I was shortly transferred, where I enjoyed a tranquil and uneventful existence, religion was still a sentiment. Being one of the older foundations we had a paid choir, and the musical service was a real delight to me. I loved the dark roof and the thunders of the organ; even now I can recollect the thrill with which I looked day after day at the pure lines of the Tudor building, the innumerable clustered shafts that ran from pavement to roof. I cared little for the archæology and history of the place, but the grace of antiquity, the walls of mellow brick, the stone-crop that dripped in purple tufts among the mouldering stones of the buttress, the very dust that clung to the rafters of the ancient refectory—all these I noted with secret thrills of delight.

Still no sense of reality touched me; life was but a moving pageant, in which I played as slight a part as I could contrive to play. I was inoffensive; my work was easy to me. I had some congenial friends, and dreamed away the weeks in a gentle indolence set in a framework of unengrossing duties.

Pleasures of Ritual
About my sixteenth year I made friends with a high-church curate whom I met in the holidays, who was indeed distantly related to me; he was attached to a large London church, which existed mainly for ornate services, and I used to go up from school occasionally to see him, and even spent a few days in his house at the beginning or end of the holidays. Looking back, he seems to me now to have been a somewhat inert and sentimental person, but I acquired from him a real love of liturgical things, wrote out with my own hand a book of Hours, carefully rubricated—though I do not recollect that I often used it—and became more ceremonial than ever. I had long settled that I was to take Orders, and I well recollect the thrill with which on one of these visits I saw my friend ascend the high stone pulpit of the tall church, with flaring lights, in a hood of a strange pattern, which he assured me was the antique shape. The sermon was, I even now recollect, deplorable both in language and thought, but that seemed to me a matter of entire indifference; the central fact was that he stood there vested with due solemnity, and made rhetorical motions with an easy grace.

A Benediction

At this time, too, at school, I took to frequenting the service of the cathedral in the town whenever I was able, and became a familiar figure to vergers and clergy. I have no doubt that were I to be made a bishop, this fact would be cited as an instance of early piety, but the truth was that it was, so to speak, a mere amusement. I can honestly say that it had no sort of effect on my life, which ran indolently on, side by side with the ritual preoccupation, unaffected by it, and indeed totally distinct from it. My confirmation came in the middle of these diversions; the solid and careful preparation that I received I looked upon as so much tedious lecturing to be decorously borne, and beside a dim pleasure in the ceremony, I do not think it had any influence of a practical kind. Once, indeed, there did pass a breath of vital truth over my placid and self-satisfied life, like a breeze over still water. There came to stay with us in the holidays an elderly clergyman, a friend of my mother's, a London rector, whose whole life was sincerely given to helping souls to the light, and who had escaped by some exquisite lucidity of soul the self-consciousness—too often, alas, the outcome of the adulation which is the shadow of holy influence. He had the gift of talking simply and sweetly about spiritual things—indeed nothing else interested him; conversation about books or politics he listened to with a gentle urbanity of tolerance; yet when he talked himself, he never dogmatised, but appealed with a wistful smile to his hearers to confirm the experiences which he related. Me, though an awkward boy, he treated with the most winning deference, and on the morning of his departure asked me with delightful grace to accompany him on a short walk, and opened to me the thought of the hallowing presence of Christ in daily life. It seems to me now that he was inviting my confidence, but I had none to give him; so with a memorable solemnity he bade me, if I ever needed help in spiritual things, to come freely to him; I remember that he did so without any sense of patronage, but as an older disciple, wrestling with the same difficulties, and only a little further ahead in the vale of life. Lastly he took me to his room, knelt down beside me, and prayed with exquisite simplicity and affection that I might be enriched with the knowledge of Christ, and then laid his hand upon my head with a loving benediction. For days and even weeks that talk and that benediction dwelt with me; but the time had not come, and I was to be led through darker waters; and though I prayed for many days intensely that some revelation of truth might come to me, yet the seed had fallen on shallow soil, and was soon scorched up again by the genial current of my daily life.

I think, though I say this with sadness, that he represented religion as too much a withdrawal from life for one so young, and did not make it clear to me that my merriment, my joys, my interests, and my ambitions might be hallowed and invigorated. He had himself subordinated life and character so completely to one end, and thrown aside (if he had ever possessed them) the dear prejudices and fiery interests of individuality, that I doubt if he could have thrown his imagination swiftly enough back into all the energetic hopes, the engrossing beckonings of opening manhood.

10

The rest of my school life passed without any important change of view. I became successful in games, popular, active-minded. I won a scholarship at Cambridge with disastrous ease.

Then Cambridge life opened before me. I speak elsewhere of my intellectual and social life there, and will pass on to the next event of importance in my religious development.

My life had become almost purely selfish. I was not very ambitious of academical honours, though I meant to secure a modest first-class; but I was intensely eager for both social and literary distinction, and submitted myself to the full to the dreamful beauty of my surroundings, and the delicious thrill of artistic pleasures.

I have often thought how strangely and secretly the crucial moment, the most agonising crisis of my life drifted upon me. I say deliberately that, looking back over my forty years of life, no day was so fraught for me with fate, no hour so big with doomful issues, as that day which dawned so simply and sped past with such familiar ease to the destined hour—that moment which waved me, led by sociable curiosity, into the darkness of suffering and agony. A new birth indeed! The current of my days fell, as it were, with suddenness, unexpected, unguessed at, into the weltering gulf of despair; that hour turned me in an instant from a careless boy into a troubled man. And yet how easily it might have been otherwise—no, I dare not say that.

The Evangelist

It had been like any other day. I had been to the dreary morning service, read huskily by a few shivering mortals in the chilly chapel; I had worked, walked in the afternoon with a friend, and we had talked of our plans—all we meant to do and be. After hall, I went to have some coffee in the rooms of a mild and amiable youth, now a church dignitary in the Colonies. I sat, I remember, on a deep sofa, which I afterwards bought and still possess. Our host carelessly said that a great Revivalist was to address a meeting that night. Some one suggested that we should go. I laughingly assented. The meeting was held in a hall in a side street; we went smiling and talking, and took our places in a crowded room. The first item was the appearance of an assistant, who accompanied the evangelist as a sort of precentor—an immense bilious man, with black hair, and eyes surrounded by flaccid, pendent, baggy wrinkles—who came forward with an unctuous gesture, and took his place at a small harmonium, placed so near the front of the platform that it looked as if both player and instrument must inevitably topple over; it was inexpressibly ludicrous to behold. Rolling his eyes in an affected manner, he touched a few simple cords, and then a marvellous transformation came over the room. In a sweet, powerful voice, with an exquisite simplicity combined with irresistible emotion, he sang "There were Ninety-and-Nine." The man was transfigured. A deathly hush came over the room, and I felt my eyes fill with tears; his physical repulsiveness slipped from him, and left a sincere impulsive Christian, whose simple music spoke straight to the heart.

Then the preacher himself—a heavy-looking, commonplace man, with a sturdy figure and no grace of look or gesture—stepped forward. I have no recollection how he began, but he had not spoken half-a-dozen sentences before I felt as though he and I were alone in the world. The details of that speech have gone from me. After a scathing and indignant invective on sin, he turned to draw a picture of the hollow, drifting life, with feeble, mundane ambitions—utterly selfish, giving no service, making no sacrifice, tasting the moment, gliding feebly down the stream of time to the roaring cataract of death. Every word he said burnt into my soul. He seemed to me to probe the secrets of my innermost heart; to be analysing, as it were, before the Judge of the world, the arid and pitiful constituents of my most secret thought. I did not think I could have heard him out … his words fell on me like the stabs of a knife. Then he made a sudden pause, and in a peroration of incredible dignity and pathos he drew us to the feet of the crucified Saviour, showed us the bleeding hand and the dimmed eye, and the infinite heart behind. "Just accept Him," he cried; "in a moment, in the twinkling of an eye, you may be His—nestling in His arms—with the burden of sin and selfishness resting at His feet."

Wounded Deep
Even as he spoke, pierced as I was to the heart by contrition and anguish, I knew that this was not for me…. He invited all who would be Christ's to wait and plead with him. Many men—even, I was surprised to

see, a careless, cynical companion of my own—crowded to the platform, but I went out into the night, like one dizzied with a sudden blow. I was joined, I remember, by a tutor of my college, who praised the eloquence of the address, and was surprised to find me so little responsive; but my only idea was to escape and be alone: I felt like a wounded creature, who must crawl into solitude. I went to my room, and after long and agonising prayers for light, an intolerable weariness fell on me, and I slept.

I awoke at some dim hour of the night in the clutch of insupportable fear; let me say at once that with the miserable weeks that followed there was mingled much of physical and nervous suffering, far more, indeed, than I then knew, or was permitted to know. I had been reading hard, and throwing myself with unaccustomed energy into a hundred new ideas and speculations. I had had a few weeks before a sudden attack of sleeplessness, which should have warned me of overstrain. But now every nervous misery known to man beset me—intolerable depression, spectral remorse, nocturnal terrors. My work was neglected. I read the Bible incessantly, and prayed for the hour together. Sometimes my depression would leave me for a few hours, like a cat playing with a mouse, and leap upon me like an evil spirit in the middle of some social gathering or harmless distraction, striking the word from my lips and the smile from my face.

For some weeks this lasted, and I think I was nearly mad. Two strange facts I will record. One day, beside myself with agitation, seeing no way out—for my prayers seemed to batter, as it were, like waves against a stony and obdurate cliff, and no hope or comfort ever slid into my soul—I wrote two letters: one to an eminent Roman Catholic, in whose sermons I had found some encouragement, and one to the elder friend I have above spoken of. In two days I received the answers. That from the Romanist hard, irritated, and bewildered—my only way was to submit myself to true direction, and he did not see that I had any intention of doing this; that it was obvious that I was being plagued for some sin which I had not ventured to open to him. I burnt the letter with a hopeless shudder. The other from my old friend, appointing a time to meet me, and saying that he understood, and that my prayers would avail.

I went soon after to see him, in a dark house in a London square. He heard me with the utmost patience, bade me believe that I was not alone in my experience; that in many a life there was—there must be—some root of bitterness that must flower before the true seed could be sown, and adding many other manly and tender things.

Liberty

He gave me certain directions, and though I will confess that I could not follow them for long—the soul must find her own path, I think, among the crags—yet he led me into a calmer, quieter, more tranquil frame of mind; he taught me that I must not expect to find the way all at once, that long coldness and habitual self-deceit must be slowly purged away. But I can never forget the infinite gratitude I owe him for the loving and strenuous way in which he brought me out into a place of liberty with the tenderness of a true father in God.

11

Thus rudely awakened to the paramount necessity of embracing a faith, bowing to a principle, obeying a gentle force which should sustain and control the soul, I flung myself for a time with ardour into theological reading, my end not erudition, but to drink at the source of life. Is it arrogant to say that I passed through a painful period of disillusionment? all round the pure well I found traces of strife and bitterness. I cast no doubt on the sincerity and zeal of those who had preceded me; but not content with drinking, and finding their eyes enlightened, they had stamped the margin of the pool into the mire, and the waters rose turbid and strife-stained to the lip. Some, like cattle on a summer evening, seemed to stand and brood within the pool itself, careless if they fouled the waters; others had built themselves booths on the margin, and sold the precious draughts in vessels of their own, enraged that any should desire the authentic stream. There was, it seemed, but little room for the wayfarer; and the very standing ground was encumbered with impotent folk.

Discerning the Faith

Not to strain a metaphor, I found that the commentators obscured rather than assisted. What I desired was to realise the character, to divine the inner thoughts of Jesus, to be fired by the impetuous eloquence of Paul, to be strengthened by the ardent simplicity of John. These critics, men of incredible diligence and patience, seemed to me to make a fence about the law, and to wrap the form I wished to see in innumerable vestments of curious design. Readers of the Protagoras of Plato will remember how the great sophist spoke from the centre of a mass of rugs and coverlets, among which, for his delectation, he lay, while the humming of his voice filled the arches of the cloister with a heavy burden of sound. I found myself in the same position as the disciples of Protagoras; the voice that I longed to hear, spoke, but it had to penetrate through the wrappings and veils which these men, in their zeal for service, had in mistaken reverence flung about the lively oracle.

A wise man said to me not long ago that the fault of teaching nowadays was that knowledge was all coined into counters; and that the desire of learners seemed to be not to possess themselves of the ore, not to strengthen and toughen the mind by the pursuit, but to possess themselves of as many of these tokens as possible, and to hand them on unchanged and unchangeable to those who came to learn of themselves.

This was my difficulty; the shelves teemed with books, the lecturers cried aloud in every College court, like the jackdaws that cawed and clanged about the venerable towers; and for a period I flew with notebook and pen from lecture to lecture, entering admirable maxims, acute verbal distinctions, ingenious parallels in my poor pages. At home I turned through book after book, and imbued myself in the learning of the schools, dreaming that, though the rind was tough, the precious morsels lay succulent within.

In this conceit of knowledge I was led to leave my College and to plunge into practical life; what my work was shall presently be related, but I will own that it was a relief. I had begun to feel that though I had learnt the use of the tools, I was no nearer finding the precious metal of which I was in search.

The further development of my faith after this cannot be told in detail, but it may be briefly sketched, after a life of some intellectual activity, not without practical employment, which has now extended over many years.

The Father
I began, I think, very far from Christ. The only vital faith that I had at first was an intense instinctive belief in the absolute power, the infinite energies, of the Father; to me he was not only Almighty, as our weak word phrases it, a Being who could, if he would, exert His power, but παντοκρατῶρ—all-conquering, all-subduing. I was led, by a process of mathematical certainty, to see that if the Father was anywhere, He was everywhere; that if He made us and bade us be, He was responsible for the smallest and most sordid details of our life and thought, as well as for the noblest and highest. It cannot indeed be otherwise; every thought and action springs from some cause, in many cases referable to events which took place in lives outside of and anterior to our own. In any case in which a man seems to enjoy the faculty of choice, his choice is in reality determined by a number of previous causes; given all the data, his action could be inevitably predicted. Thus I gradually realised that sin in the moral world, and disease

in the physical, are each of them some manifestation of the Eternal Will. If He gives to me the joy of life, the energy of action, did He not give it to the subtle fungus, to the venomous bacteria which, once established in our bodies, are known by the names of cancer and fever? Why all life should be this uneasy battle I know not; but if we can predicate consciousness of any kind to these strange rudiments, the living slime of the pit, is it irreverent to say that faith may play a part in their work as well? When the health-giving medicine pours along our veins, what does it mean but that everywhere it leaves destruction behind it, and that the organisms of disease which have, with delighted zest, been triumphing in their chosen dwelling and rioting in the instinctive joy of life, sadly and mutely resign the energy that animates them, or sink into sleep. It is all a balance, a strife, a battle. Why such striving and fighting, such uneasy victory and deep unrest should be the Father's will for all His creatures, I know not; but that it is a condition, a law of His own mind, I can reverently believe. When we sing the Benedicite, which I for one do with all my heart, we must be conscious that it is only a selection, after all, of phenomena that are impressive, delightful, or useful to ourselves. Nothing that we call, God forgive us, noxious, finds a place there. St. Francis, indeed, went further, and praised God for "our sister the Death of the Body," but in the larger Benedicite of the universe, which is heard by the ear of God, the fever and the pestilence, the cobra and the graveyard worm utter their voices too; and who shall say that the Father hears them not?

The Joy of the World
If one believes that happiness is inch by inch diminishing, that it is all a losing fight, then it must be granted that we have no refuge but in a Stoic hardening of the heart; but when we look at life and see the huge preponderance of joy over pain—such tracts of healthy energy, sweet duty, quiet movement—indeed when we see, as we often do, the touching spectacle of hope and joy again and again triumphant over weakness and weariness; when we see such unselfishness abroad, such ardent desire to lighten the loads of others and to bear their burdens; then it is faithless indeed if we allow ourselves to believe that the Father has any end in view but the ultimate happiness of all the innumerable units, which He endows with independent energies, and which, one by one, after their short taste of this beautiful and exquisite world, resign their powers again, often so gladly, into His hand.

Our Insignificance
But the fault, if I may so phrase it, of this faith, is the vastness of the conception to which it opens the mind. When I contemplate this earth with its continents and islands, its mountains and plains, all stored with histories of life and death, the bones of dead monsters, the shattered hulks of time;

the vast briny ocean with all the mysterious life that stirs beneath the heaving crests; when I realise that even this world, with all its infinite records of life, is but a speck in the heavens, and that every one of the suns of space may be surrounded with the same train of satellites, in which some tumultuous drama of life may be, nay, must be enacting itself—that even on the fiery orbs themselves some appalling Titan forms may be putting forth their prodigious energies, suffering and dying—the mind of man reels before the thought;—and yet all is in the mind of God. The consciousness of the microscopic minuteness of my own life and energies, which yet are all in all to me, becomes crushing and paralysing in the light of such a thought. It seems impossible to believe, in the presence of such a spectacle, that the single life can have any definite importance, and the temptation comes to resign all effort, to swim on the stream, just planning life to be as easy and as pleasant as possible, before one sinks into the abyss.

12
From such a paralysis of thought and life two beliefs have saved me.

The Master
First, it may be confessed, came the belief in the Spirit of God, the thought of inner holiness, not born from any contemplation of the world around, which seems indeed to point to far different ideals. Yet as true and truer than the bewildering example of nature is the inner voice which speaks, after the wind and storm, in the silent solitudes of the soul. That this voice exists and is heard can admit of no tangible demonstration; each must speak for himself; but experience forbids me to doubt that there is something which contradicts the seduction of appetite, something which calls, as it were, a flush to the face of the soul at the thought of triumphs of sense, a voice that without being derisive or harsh, yet has a terrible and instantaneous severity; and wields a mental scourge, the blows of which are no less fearful to receive because they are accompanied with no physical disaster. To recognise this voice as the very voice and word of the Father to sentient souls, is the inevitable result of experience and thought.

Then came the triumphant belief, weak at first, but taking slow shape, that the attitude of the soul to its Maker can be something more than a distant reverence, an overpowering awe, a humble worship; the belief, the certainty that it can be, as it were, a personal link—that we can indeed hold converse with God, speak with Him, call upon Him, put to use a human phrase, our hand in His, only desiring to be led according to His will.

Then came the further step; after some study of the systems of other teachers of humanity, after a desire to find in the great redeemers of mankind, in Buddha, Socrates, Mahomet, Confucius, Shakespeare, the secret of self-conquest, of reconciliation, the knowledge slowly dawns upon the mind that in Jesus of Galilee alone we are in the presence of something which enlightens man not from within but from without. The other great teachers of humanity seem to have looked upon the world and into their own hearts, and deduced from thence, by flashes of indescribable genius, some order out of the chaos, some wise and temperate scheme, but with Jesus—though I long resisted the conviction—it is different. He comes, not as a man speaking by observation and thought, but as a visitant from some secret place, who knows the truth rather than guesses at it. I need not say that his reporters, the Gospel writers, had but an imperfect conception of His majesty. His ineffable greatness—it could not well be otherwise; the mystery rather is that with such simple views of life, such elementary conceptions of the scheme of things, they yet gave so much of the stupendous truth, and revealed Jesus in his words and acts as the Divine Man, who spoke to man not by spiritual influences but by the very authentic utterance of God. Such teaching as the parables, such scenes as the raising of Lazarus, or the midday talk by the wayside well of Sychar, emerge from all art and history with a dignity that lays no claim to the majesty that they win; and as the tragedy darkens and thickens to its close, such scenes as the trial, recorded by St. John, and the sacred death, bring home to the mind the fact that no mere humanity could bear itself with such gentle and tranquil dignity, such intense and yet such unselfish suffering as were manifested in the Son of Man.

The Return
And so, as the traveller goes out and wanders through the cities of men, among stately palaces, among the glories of art, or climbs among the aching solitudes of lonely mountains, or feasts his eyes upon green isles floating in sapphire seas, and returns to find that the old strait dwelling-place, the simple duties of life, the familiar friends, homely though they be, are the true anchors of the spirit; so, after a weary pilgrimage, the soul comes back, with glad relief, with wistful tenderness, to the old beliefs of childhood, which, in its pride and stubbornness, it cast aside, and rejected as weak and inadequate and faded; finds after infinite trouble and weariness that it has but learnt afresh what it knew; and that though the wanderer has ransacked the world, digged and drunk strange waters, trafficked for foreign merchandise, yet the Pearl of Price, the White Stone is hidden after all in his own garden-ground, and inscribed with his own new name.

13
I need not enter very closely into the period of my life which followed the university. After a good deal of hesitation and uncertainty I decided to enter for the Home Civil Service, and obtained a post in a subordinate office. The work I found not wholly uninteresting, but it needs no special record here. I acquired the knowledge of how to conduct business, a certain practical power of foreseeing contingencies, a certain acquaintance with legal procedure, and some knowledge of human nature in its official aspect.

Intellectually and morally this period of my life was rather stagnant. I had been through a good deal of excitement, of mental and moral malady, of general bouleversement. Nature exacted a certain amount of quiescence, melancholy quiescence for the most part, because I felt myself singularly without energy to carry out my hopes and schemes, and at the same time it seemed that time was ebbing away purposelessly, and that I was not driving, so to speak, any piles in the fluid and oozy substratum of ideas on which my life seemed built. To revel in metaphors, I was like a snake which has with a great strain bolted a quadruped, and needs a long space of uneasy and difficult digestion. But at the time I did not see this; I only thought I was losing time: I felt with Milton—

"How soon hath time, the subtle thief of youth,
Stolen on his wing my three-and-twentieth year."

But beset as I was by the sublime impatience of youth, I had not serenity enough to follow out the thoughts which Milton works out in the rest of the sonnet.

Literary Work
At the same time, so far as literary work went, to which I felt greatly drawn, I was not so impatient. I wrote a great deal for my private amusement, and to practise facility of expression, but with little idea of hurried publication. A story which I sent to a well-known editor was courteously returned to me, with a letter in which he stated that he had read my work carefully, and that he felt it a duty to tell me that it was "sauce without meat." This kind and wholesome advice made a great difference to me; I determined that I would attempt to live a little before I indulged in baseless generalisation, or lectured other people on the art of life. I soon gained great facility in writing, and developed a theory, which I have ever since had no reason to doubt, that performance is simply a matter of the intensity of desire. If one only wants enough to complete a definite piece of work, be it poem, essay, story, or some far more definite and prosaic task, I have found that it gets itself done in spite of the insistent pressure of other

businesses and the deadening monotony of heavy routine, simply because one goes back to it with delight, schemes to clear time for it, waits for it round corners, and loses no time in spurring and whipping the mind to work, which is necessary in the case of less attractive tasks. The moment that there comes a leisurely gap, the mind closes on the beloved work like a limpet; when this happens day after day and week after week, the accumulations become prodigious.

I thus felt gradually more and more, that when the magnum opus did present itself to be done, I should probably be able to carry it through; and meanwhile I had sufficient self-respect, although I suffered twinges of thwarted ambition, not to force my crude theories, my scrambling prose, or my faltering verse upon the world.

London
Meanwhile I lived a lonely sort of life, with two or three close intimates. I never really cared for London, but it is at the same time idle to deny its fascination. In the first place it is full from day to day of prodigious, astounding, unexpected beauties—sometimes beauty on a noble scale, in the grand style, such as when the sunset shakes its hair among ragged clouds, and the endless leagues of house-roofs and the fronts of town palaces dwindle into a far-off steely horizon-line under the huge and wild expanse of sky. Sometimes it is the smaller, but no less alluring beauty of subtle atmospherical effects; and so conventional is the human appreciation of beauty that the constant presence, in these London pictures, of straight framing lines, contributed by house-front and street-end, is an aid to the imagination. Again, there is the beauty of contrasts; the vignettes afforded by the sudden blossoming of rustic flowers and shrubs in unexpected places; the rustle of green leaves at the end of a monotonous street. And then, apart from natural beauty, there is the vast, absorbing, incredible pageant of humanity, full of pathos, of wistfulness, and of sweetness. But of this I can say but little; for it always moved me, and moves me yet, with a sort of horror. I think it was always to me a spectacular interest; I never felt one with the human beings whom I watched, or even in the same boat, so to speak, with them; the contemplation of the fact that I am one of so many millions has been to me a humiliating rather than an inspiring thought; it dashes the pleasures of individuality; it arraigns the soul before a dark and inflexible bar. Passing daily through London, there is little possibility in the case of an imaginative man for hopeful expansion of the heart, little ground for anything but an acquiescent acceptance. Under these conditions it is too rudely brought home to me to be wholesome, how ineffective, undistinguished, typical, minute, uninteresting any one human being is after all: and though the sight of humanity in every form is attractive, bewildering,

painfully interesting, thrilling, and astounding—though one finds unexpected beauty and goodness everywhere—yet I recognise that city life had a deadening effect on my consciousness, and hindered rather than helped the development of thought and life.

The Artist

Still, in other ways this period was most valuable—it made me practical instead of fanciful; alert instead of dreamy; it made me feel what I had never known before, the necessity for grasping the exact point of a matter, and not losing oneself among side issues. It helped me out of the entirely amateurish condition of mind into which I had been drifting—and, moreover, it taught me one thing which I had never realised, a lesson for which I am profoundly grateful, namely that literature and art play a very small part in the lives of the majority of people; that most men have no sort of an idea that they are serious matters, but look upon them as more or less graceful amusements; that in such regions they have no power of criticism, and no judgment; but that these are not nearly such serious defects as the defect of vision which the artist and the man of letters suffer from and encourage—the defect, I mean, of treating artistic ideals as matters of pre-eminent national, even of moral importance. They must be content to range themselves frankly with other craftsmen; they may sustain themselves by thinking that they may help, a very little, to ameliorate conditions, to elevate the tone of morality and thought, to provide sources of recreation, to strengthen the sense of beauty; but they must remember that they cannot hope to belong to the primal and elemental things of life. Not till the primal needs are satisfied does the work of the poet and artist begin—"After the banquet, the minstrel."

The poet and the artist too often live, like the Lady of Shalott, weaving a magic web of fair and rich colour, but dealing not with life itself, and not even with life viewed ipsis oculis, but in the magic mirror. The Lady of Shalott is doubly secluded from the world; she does not mingle with it, she does not even see it; so the writer sometimes does not even see the life which he describes, but draws his knowledge secondhand, through books and bookish secluded talk. I do not think that I under-rate the artistic vocation; but it is only one of many, and, though different in kind, certainly not superior to the vocations of those who do the practical work of the world.

From this dangerous heresy I was saved just at the moment when it was waiting to seize upon me, and at a time when a man's convictions are apt to settle themselves for life, by contact with the prosaic, straightforward and commonplace world.

At one time I saw a certain amount of society; my father's old friends were very kind to me, and I was thus introduced to what is a far more interesting circle of society than the circle which would rank itself highest, and which spends an amount of serious toil in the search of amusement, with results which to an outsider appear to be unsatisfactory. The circle to which I gained admittance was the official set—men who had definite and interesting work in the world—barristers, government officials, politicians and the like, men versed in affairs, and with a hard and definite knowledge of what was really going on. Here I learnt how different is the actual movement of politics from the reflection of it which appears in the papers, which often definitely conceals the truth from the public.

Diversions

My amusements at this period were of the mildest character; I spent Sundays in the summer months at Golden End; Sundays in the winter as a rule at my lodgings; and devoted the afternoons on which I was free, to long aimless rambles in London, or even farther afield. I have an absurd pleasure in observing the details of domestic architecture; and there is a variety of entertainment to be derived, for a person with this low and feeble taste, from the exploration of London, which would probably be inconceivable to persons of a more conscientious artistic standard.

A Rude Shock

At this period I had few intimates; and sociable as I had been at school and college, I was now thrown far more on my own resources; I sometimes think it was a wise and kindly preparation for what was coming; and I certainly learnt the pleasures to be derived from reading and lonely contemplation and solitary reflection, pleasures which have stood me in good stead in later days. I used indeed to think that the enforced spending of so many hours of the day with other human beings gave a peculiar zest to these solitary hours. Whether this was wholesome or natural I know not, but I certainly enjoyed it, and lived for several years a life of interior speculation which was neither sluggish nor morbid. I learnt my business thoroughly, and in all probability I should have settled down quietly and comfortably to the life of a bachelor official, rotating from chambers to office and from office to club, had it not been that just at the moment when I was beginning to crystallise into sluggish, comfortable habits, I was flung by a rude shock into a very different kind of atmosphere.

14
The Doctor

I must now relate, however briefly, the event which once for all determined the conditions of my present life. For the last six months of my professional work I had been feeling indefinitely though not decidedly unwell. I found myself disinclined to exertion, bodily or mental, easily elated, easily depressed, at times strangely somnolent, at others irritably wakeful; at last some troublesome symptoms warned me that I had better put myself in the hands of a doctor. I went to a local practitioner whose account disquieted me; he advised me to apply to an eminent specialist, which I accordingly did.

The Verdict

I am not likely to forget the incidents of that day. I went up to London, and made my way to the specialist's house. After a dreary period of waiting, in a dark room looking out on a blank wall, the table abundantly furnished with periodicals whose creased and battered aspect betokened the nervous handling to which they had been subjected, I was at last summoned to the presence of the great man himself. He presented an appearance of imperturbable good-nature; his rosy cheeks, his little snub nose, his neatly groomed appearance, his gold-rimmed spectacles, wore an air of commonplace prosperity that was at once reassuring. He asked me a number of questions, made a thorough examination, writing down certain details in a huge volume, and finally threw himself back in his chair with a deliberate air that somewhat disconcerted me. At last my sentence came. I was undoubtedly suffering from the premonitory symptoms of a serious, indeed dangerous complaint, and I must at once submit myself to the condition of an invalid life. He drew out a table diet, and told me to live a healthy, quiet life under the most restful conditions attainable. He asked me about my circumstances, and I told him with as much calmness as I could muster. He replied that I was very fortunate, that I must at once give up professional work and be content to vegetate. "Mind," he said, "I don't want you to be bored—that will be as bad for you as to be overworked. But you must avoid all kinds of worry and fatigue—all extremes. I should not advise you to travel at present, if you like a country life—in fact I should say, live the life that attracts you, apart from any professional exertions; don't do anything you don't like. Now, Mr. ———," he continued, "I have told you the worst— the very worst. I can't say whether your constitution will triumph over this complaint: to be candid, I do not think it will; but there is no question of any immediate risk whatever. Indeed, if you were dependent on your own exertions for a livelihood, I could promise you some years of work—though that would render it almost impossible for you ever to recover. As it is, you may consider that you have a chance of entire recovery, and if you can follow my directions, and no unforeseen complications intervene, I think you may look forward to a fairly long life; but mind that any work you do must be of the nature of amusement. Once and for all, strain of any sort is out of the question, and if you indulge in any excessive or exciting exertions, you will inevitably shorten your life. There, I have told you a disagreeable truth—make the best of it—remember that I see many people every week who have to bear far more distressing communications. You had better come to see me every three months, unless you have any marked symptoms, such as"—(there followed medical details with which I need not trouble the reader)—"in that case come to me at once; but I tell you plainly that I do not anticipate them. You seem to have what I call the patient temperament—to have a vocation, if I may say so," (here he smiled benevolently) "for the invalid life." He rose as he spoke, shook hands kindly, and opened the door.

15
New Perceptions
I will confess that at first this communication was a great shock to me; I was for a time bewildered and plunged into a deep dejection. To say farewell to the bustle and activity of life—to be laid aside on a shelf, like a cracked vase, turning as far as possible my ornamental front to the world, spoilt for homely service. To be relegated to the failures; to be regarded and spoken of as an invalid—to live the shadowed life, a creature of rules and hours, fretting over drugs and beef tea—a degrading, a humiliating rôle. I admit that the first weeks of my enforced retirement were bitter indeed. The perpetual fret of small restrictions had at first the effect of making me feel physically and mentally incapable. Only very gradually did the sad cloud lift. The first thing that came to my help was a totally unexpected feeling. When I had got used to the altered conditions of life, when I found that the regulated existence had become to a large extent mechanical, when I had learnt to decide instinctively what I could attempt and what I must leave alone, I found my perceptions curiously heightened and intensified by the shadowy background which enveloped me. Sounds and sights thrilled me in an unaccustomed way—the very thought, hardly defined, but existing like a quiet subconsciousness, that my tenure of life was certainly frail, and might be brief, seemed to bring out into sharp relief the simple and unnoticed sensations of ordinary life. The pure gush of morning air through the opened casement, the delicious coolness of water on the languid body, the liquid song of birds, the sprouting of green buds upon the hedge, the sharp and aromatic scent of rosy larch tassels, the monotonous babble of the stream beneath its high water plants, the pearly laminæ of the morning cloudland, the glowing wrack of sunset with the liquid bays of intenser green—all these stirred my spirit with an added value of beauty, an

enjoyment at once passionate and tranquil, as though they held some whispered secret for the soul.

The same quickening effect passed, I noticed, over intellectual perceptions. Pictures in which there was some latent quality, some hidden brooding, some mystery lying beneath and beyond superficial effect, gave up their secrets to my eye. Music came home to me with an intensity of pathos and passion which I had before never even suspected, and even here the same subtle power of appreciation seemed to have been granted me. It seemed that I was no longer taken in by technical art or mechanical perfection. The hard rippling cascades which had formerly attracted me, where a musician was merely working out, if I may use the word, some subject with a mathematical precision, seemed to me hollow and vain; all that was pompous and violent followed suit, and what I now seemed to be able to discern was all that endeavoured, however faultily, to express some ardour of the spirit, some indefinable delicacy of feeling.

Something of the same power seemed to be mine in dealing with literature. All hard brilliance, all exaggerated display, all literary agility and diplomacy that might have once deceived me, appeared to ring cracked and thin; mere style, style that concealed rather than expressed thought, fell as it were in glassy tingling showers on my initiated spirit; while, on the other hand, all that was truthfully felt, sincerely conceived or intensely desired, drew me as with a magical compulsion. It was then that I first perceived what the sympathy, the perception born of suffering might be, when that suffering was not so intrusive, so severe, as to throw the sick spirit back upon itself—then that I learnt what detachment, what spectatorial power might be conferred by a catastrophe not violent, but sure, by a presage of distant doom. I felt like a man who has long stumbled among intricate lanes, his view obscured by the deep-cut earth-walls of his prison, and by the sordid lower slopes with their paltry details, when the road leads out upon the open moor, and when at last he climbs freely and exultingly upon the broad grassy shoulders of the hill. The true perspective—the map of life opened out before me; I learnt that all art is only valuable when it is the sedulous flowering of the sweet and gracious spirit, and that beyond all power of human expression lies a province where the deepest thoughts, the highest mysteries of the spirit sleep—only guessed at, wrestled with, hankered after by the most skilled master of all the arts of mortal subtlety.

Perhaps the very thing that made these fleeting impressions so perilously sweet, was the sense of their evanescence.

> But oh, the very reason why
> I love them, is because they die.

The Shadow

In this exalted mood, with this sense of heightened perception all about me, I began for awhile to luxuriate. I imagined that I had learnt a permanent lesson, gained a higher level of philosophy, escaped from the grip of material things. Alas! it was but transitory. I had not triumphed. What I did gain, what did stay with me, was a more deliberate intention of enjoying simple things, a greater expectation of beauty in homely life. This remained, but in a diminished degree. I suppose that the mood was one of intense nervous tension, for by degrees it was shadowed and blotted, until I fell into a profound depression. At best what could I hope for?—a shadowed life, an inglorious gloom? The dull waste years stretched before me—days, weeks, months of wearisome little duties; dreary tending of the lamp of life; and what a life! life without service, joy, brightness, or usefulness. I was to be stranded like a hulk on an oozy shore, only thankful for every month that the sodden timbers still held together. I saw that something larger and deeper was required; I saw that religion and philosophy must unite to form some definite theory of life, to build a foundation on which I could securely rest.

16

The service of others, in some form or another, must sustain me. Philosophy pointed out that to narrow my circle every year, to turn the microscope of thought closer and closer upon my frail self, would be to sink month by month deeper into egotism and self-pity. Religion gave a more generous impulse still.

Beginnings

What is our duty with respect to philanthropy? It is obviously absurd to think that every one is bound to tie themselves hand and foot to some thoroughly uncongenial task. Fitness and vocation must come in. Clergy, doctors, teachers are perhaps the most obvious professional philanthropists; for either of the two latter professions I was incapacitated. Some hovering thought of attempting to take orders, and to become a kind of amateur, unprofessional curate, visited me; but my religious views made that difficult, and the position of a man who preaches what he does not wholly believe is inconsistent with self-respect. Christianity as taught by the sects seemed to me to have drifted hopelessly away from the detached simplicity inculcated by Christ; to have become a mere part of the social system, fearfully invaded and overlaid by centuries of unintelligent tradition. To work, for instance, even with Mr. Woodward, at his orders, on his system, would have been an impossibility both for him and for myself. I had, besides, a strong feeling that work, to be of use, must be done, not in a spirit of complacent self-satisfaction, but at least with some energy of enjoyment, some conviction. It seemed moreover clear that, for a time at all events, my place and position in the world was settled: I must live a quiet home life, and endeavour, at all events, to restore some measure of effective health. How could I serve my neighbours best? They were mostly quiet country people—a few squires and clergy, a few farmers, and many farm labourers. Should I accept a country life as my sphere, or was I bound to try and find some other outlet for whatever effectiveness I possessed? I came deliberately to the conclusion that I was not only not bound to go elsewhere, but that it was the most sensible, wisest, and Christian solution to stay where I was and make some experiments.

My Schemes

The next practical difficulty was how I could help. English people have a strong sense of independence. They would neither understand nor value a fussy, dragooning philanthropist, who bustled about among them, finding fault with their domestic arrangements, lecturing, dictating. I determined that I would try to give them the help they wanted; not the help I thought they ought to want. That I would go among them with no idea of improving, but of doing, if possible, neighbourly and unobtrusive kindnesses, and that under no circumstances would I diminish their sense of independence by weak generosity.

About this time, my mother at luncheon happened to mention that the widow of a small farmer, who was living in a cottage not fifty yards from our gate, was in trouble about her eldest boy, who was disobedient, idle, and unsatisfactory. He had been employed by more than one neighbour in garden work, but had lost two places by laziness and impertinence. Here was a point d'appui. In the afternoon I strolled across; nervous and shy, I confess, to a ridiculous degree. I knew the woman by sight, and little more. I felt thoroughly unfitted for my rôle, and feared that patronage would be resented. However, I went and found Mrs. Dewhurst at home. I was received with real geniality and something of delicate sympathy—the news of my illness had got about. I determined I would ask no leading questions, but bit by bit her anxieties were revealed: the boy was a trouble to her. "What did he want?" She didn't know; but he was discontented and naughty, had got into bad company. I asked if it would be any good my seeing the boy, and found that it would evidently be a relief. I asked her to send the boy to me that evening, and went away with a real and friendly handshake, and an invitation to come again. In the evening Master Dewhurst turned up—a shy, uninteresting, rather insolent boy, strong and well-built, and with a world of energy in his black eyes. I asked him what he wanted to do, and after a little talk it all came out: he was sick of the place; he did not want garden work. "What would he do? What did he like?" I found that he wanted to see something of the world. Would he go to sea? The boy brightened up at once, and then said he didn't want to leave his mother. Our interview closed, and this necessitated my paying a further call on the mother, who was most sensible, and evidently felt that what the boy wanted was a thorough change.

To make a long story short, it cost me a few letters and a very little money, defined as a loan; the boy went off to a training ship, and after a few weeks found that he had the very life he wanted; indeed, he is now a promising young sailor, who never fails to write to me at intervals, and who comes to see me whenever he comes home. The mother is a firm friend. Now that I am at my ease with her, I am astonished at the shrewdness and sense of her talk.

It would be tedious to recount, as I could, fifty similar adventures; my enterprises include a village band, a cricket club, a co-operative store; but the personal work, such as it is, has broadened every year: I am an informal adviser to thirty or forty families, and the correspondence entailed, to say nothing of my visits, gives me much pleasant occupation. The circle now insensibly widens; I do not pretend that there are not times of weariness, and even disagreeable experiences connected with it. I am a poor hand in a sick-room, I confess it with shame; my mother, who is not particularly interested in her neighbours, is ten times as effective.

The Reward

But what I feel most strongly about the whole, is the intense interest which has grown up about it. The trust which these simple folk repose in me is the factor which rescues me from the indolent impulse to leave matters alone; even if I desired to do so, I could not for very shame disappoint them. Moreover, I cannot pretend that it takes up very much time. The institutions run themselves for the most part. I don't overdo my visits; indeed, I seldom go to call on my friends unless there is something specific to be done. But I am always at home for them between seven and eight. My downstairs smoking-room, once an office, has a door which opens on the drive, so that it is not necessary for these Nicodemite visitors to come through the house. Sometimes for days together I have no one; sometimes I have three or four callers in the evening. I don't talk religion as a rule, unless I am asked; but we discuss politics and local matters with avidity. I have persistently refused to take any office, and I fear that our neighbours think me a very lazy kind of dilettante, who happens to be interested in the small-talk of rustics. I will not be a Guardian, as I have little turn for business; and when it was suggested to me that I might be a J. P., I threw cold water on the scheme. Any official position would alter my relation to my friends, and I should often be put in a difficulty; but by being absolutely unattached, I find that confidential dealings are made easy.

I fear that this will sound a very shabby, unromantic, and gelatinous form of philanthropy, and I am quite unable to defend it on utilitarian principles. I can only say that it is deeply absorbing; that it pays, so to speak, a large interest on a small investment of trouble, and that it has given me a sense of perspective in human things which I never had before. The difficulty in writing about it is to abstain from platitudes; I can only say that it has revealed to me how much more emotion and experience go to make up a platitude than I ever suspected before in my ambitious days.

17

Ennui is, after all, the one foe that we all fear; and in arranging our life, the most serious preoccupation is how to escape it. The obvious reply is, of course, "plenty of cheerful society." But is not general society to a man with a taste for seclusion the most irritating, wearing, ennuyeux method of filling the time? It is not the actual presence of people that is distressing, though that in some moods is unbearable, but it is the consciousness of duties towards them, whether as host or guest, that sits, like the Old Man of the Sea, upon one's shoulders. A considerable degree of seclusion can be attained by a solitary-minded man at a large hotel. The only time of the day when you are compelled to be gregarious is the table d'hôte dinner; and then, even if you desire to talk, it is often made impossible by the presence of foreigners among whom one is sandwiched. But take a visit at a large English country-house; a mixed party with possibly little in common; the protracted meals, the vacuous sessions, the interminable promenades. Men are better off than women in this respect, as at most periods of the year they are swept off in the early forenoon to some vigorous employment, and are not expected to return till tea-time. But take such a period in August, a month in which many busy men are compelled to pay visits if they pay them at all. Think of the desultory cricket matches, the futile gabble of garden parties.

Of course the desire of solitude, or rather, the nervous aversion to company, may become so intense as to fall under the head of monomania;

doctors give it an ugly name, I know not exactly what it is, like the agoraphobia, which is one of the subsections of a certain form of madness. Agoraphobia is the nervous horror of crowds, which causes persons afflicted by it to swoon away at the prospect of having to pass through a square or street crowded with people.

But the dislike of visitors is a distinct, but quite as specific form of nervous mania. One lady of whom I have heard was in the habit of darting to the window and involving herself in the window-curtain the moment she heard a ring at the bell; another, more secretive still, crept under the sofa. Not so very long ago I went over a great house in the North; my host took me to a suite of upper rooms with a charming view. "These," he said, "were inhabited by my old aunt Susan till her death some months ago; she was somewhat eccentric in her habits"—here he thrust his foot under a roomy settee which stood in the window, and to my intense surprise a bell rang loudly underneath—"Ah," he said, rather shamefacedly, "they haven't taken it off." I begged for an explanation, and he said that the old lady had formed an inveterate habit of creeping under the settee the moment she heard a knock at the door; to cure her of it, they hung a bell on a spring beneath it, so that she gave warning of her whereabouts.

Solitude

Society is good for most of us; but solitude is equally good, as a tonic medicine, granted that sociability is accepted as a factor in our life. A certain deliberate solitude, like the fast days in the Roman Church, is useful, even if only by way of contrast, and that we may return with fresh zest to ordinary intercourse.

People who are used to sociable life find the smallest gap, the smallest touch of solitude oppressive and ennuyeux; and it may be taken for granted that the avoidance of ennui, in whatever form that whimsical complaint makes itself felt, is one of the most instinctive prepossessions of the human race; but it does not follow that solitude should not be resolutely practised; and any sociable person who has strength of mind to devote, say, one day of the week to absolute and unbroken loneliness would find not only that such times would come to have a positive value of their own, but that they would enhance infinitely the pleasures of social life.

It is a curious thing how fast the instinct for solitude grows. A friend of mine, a clergyman, a man of an inveterately sociable disposition, was compelled by the exigencies of his position to take charge of a lonely sea-coast parish, the incumbent of which had fallen desperately ill. The parish was not very populous, and extremely scattered; the nearest houses, inhabited by educated people were respectively four and five miles away—my friend was poor, an indifferent walker, and had no vehicle at his command.

He went off, he told me, with extreme and acute depression. He found a small rectory-house with three old silent servants. He established himself there with his books, and began in a very heavy-hearted way to discharge the duties of the position; he spent his mornings in quiet reading or strolling—the place lay at the top of high cliffs and included many wild and magnificent prospects. The afternoon he spent in trudging over the parish, making himself acquainted with the farmers and other inhabitants of the region. In the evening he read and wrote again. He had not been there a week before he became conscious that the life had a charm. He had written in the first few days of his depression to several old friends imploring them to have mercy on his loneliness. Circumstances delayed their arrival, and at last when he had been there some six weeks, a letter announcing the arrival of an old friend and his wife for a week's visit gave him, he confessed, far more annoyance than pleasure. He entertained them, however, but felt distinctly relieved when they departed. At the end of the six months I saw him, and he told me that solitude was a dangerous Circe, seductive, delicious, but one that should be resolutely and deliberately shunned, an opiate of which one could not estimate the fascination. And I am not speaking of a torpid or indolent man, but a man of force, intellect, and cultivation, of a restless mind and vivid interests.

[The passages that follow were either extracted by the author himself from his own diaries, or are taken from a notebook containing fragments of an autobiographical character. When the date is ascertainable it is given at the head of the piece.—J. T.

18
Now I will draw, carefully, faithfully, and lovingly, the portraits of some of my friends; they are not ever likely to set eyes on the delineation: and if by some chance they do, they will forgive me, I think.

I have chosen three or four of the most typical of my not very numerous neighbours, though there are many similar portraits scattered up and down my diaries.

It happened this morning that a small piece of parish business turned up which necessitated my communicating with Sir James, our chief landowner. Staunton is his name, and his rank is baronet. He comes from a typically English stock. As early as the fourteenth century the Stauntons seem to have held land in the parish; they were yeomen, no doubt, owning a few hundred acres of freehold. In the sixteenth century one of them drifted to London, made a fortune, and, dying childless, left his money to the head of the house, who bought more land, built a larger house, became esquire, and eventually knight; his brass is in the church. They were unimaginative folk, and whenever the country was divided, they generally contrived to find themselves upon the prosaic and successful side.

The Bishop
Early in the eighteenth century there were two brothers: the younger, a clergyman, by some happy accident became connected with the Court, made a fortunate marriage, and held a deanery first, and then a bishopric. Here he amassed a considerable fortune. His portrait, which hangs at the Park, represents a man with a face of the shape and colour of a ripe plum, with hardly more distinction of feature, shrouded in a full wig. Behind him, under a velvet curtain, stands his cathedral, in a stormy sky. The bishop's monument is one of the chief disfigurements, or the chief ornaments of our church, according as your taste is severe or catholic. It represents the deceased prelate in a reclining attitude, with a somewhat rueful expression, as of a man fallen from a considerable height. Over him bends a solicitous angel in the attitude of one inquiring what is amiss. One of the prelate's delicate hands is outstretched from a gigantic lawn sleeve, like a haggis, which requires an iron support to sustain it; the other elbow is propped upon some marble volumes of controversial divinity. In an alcove behind is a tumid mitre, quite putting into the shade a meagre celestial crown with marble rays, which is pushed unceremoniously into the top of the recess.

The Baronets
The bishop succeeded his elder brother in the estate, and added largely to the property. The bishop's only son sat for a neighbouring borough, and was created a baronet for his services, which were of the most straightforward kind. At this point, by one of the strange freaks of which even county families are sometimes guilty, a curious gleam of romance flashed across the dull record. The baronet's eldest son developed dim literary tastes, drifted to London, became a hanger-on of the Johnsonian circle—his name occurs in footnotes to literary memoirs of the period; married a lady of questionable reputation, and published two volumes of "Letters to a Young Lady of Quality," which combine, to a quite singular degree, magnificence of diction with tenuity of thought. This Jack Staunton was a spendthrift, and would have made strange havoc of the estate, but his father fortunately outlived him; and by the offer of a small pension to Mrs.

Jack, who was left hopelessly destitute, contrived to get the little grandson and heir into his own hands. The little boy developed into the kind of person that no one would desire as a descendant, but that all would envy as an ancestor. He was a miser pure and simple. In his day the tenants were ground down, rents were raised, plantations were made, land was acquired in all directions; but the house became ruinous, and the miserable owner, in a suit of coarse cloth like a second-rate farmer, sneaked about his lands with a shy and secret smile, avoiding speech with tenants and neighbours alike, and eating small and penurious meals in the dusty dining-room in company with an aged and drunken bailiff, the discovery of whose constant attempts to defraud his master of a few shillings were the delight and triumph of the baronet's life. He died a bachelor; at his death a cousin, a grandson of the first baronet, succeeded, and found that whatever else he had done, the miser had left immense accumulations of money behind him. This gentleman was in the army, and fought at Waterloo, after which he imitated the example of his class, and became an unflinching Tory politician. The fourth baronet was a singularly inconspicuous person whom I can just remember, whose principal diversion was his kennel. I have often seen him when, as a child, I used to lunch there with my mother, stand throughout the meal in absolute silence, sipping a glass of sherry on the hearthrug, and slowly munching a large biscuit, and, before we withdrew, producing from his pocket the envelopes which had contained the correspondence of the morning, and filling them with bones, pieces of fat, fag-ends of joints, to bestow upon the dogs in the course of the afternoon. This habit I considered, as a child, to be distinctly agreeable, and I should have been deeply disappointed if Sir John had ever failed to do it.

Sir James

The present Sir James is now a man of forty. He was at Eton and Trinity, and for a short time in the Guards. He married the daughter of a neighbouring baronet, and at the age of thirty, when his father died, settled down to the congenial occupation of a country gentleman. He is, in spite of the fact that he had a large landed estate, a very wealthy man. I imagine he has at least £20,000 a year. He has a London house, to which Lady Staunton goes for the season, but Sir James, who makes a point of accompanying her, soon finds that business necessitates his at once returning to the country; and I am not sure that the summer months, which he spends absolutely alone, are not the most agreeable part of the year for him. He has three stolid and healthy children—two boys and a girl. He takes no interest whatever in politics, religion, literature, or art. He takes in the Standard and the Field. He hunts a little, and shoots a little, but does not care about either. He spends his morning and afternoon in pottering about the estate. In the evening he writes a few letters, dines well, reads the paper and goes to bed.

He does not care about dining out; indeed the prospect of a dinner-party or a dance clouds the pleasure of the day. He goes to church once on Sunday; he is an active magistrate; he has, at long intervals, two or three friends of like tastes to stay with him, who accompany him, much to his dislike, in his perambulations, and stand about whistling, or staring at stacks and cattle, while he talks to the bailiff. But he is a kindly, cheery, generous man, with a good head for business, and an idea of his position. He is absolutely honourable and straightforward, and faces an unpleasant duty, when he has made up his mind to it, with entire tranquillity. No mental speculation has ever come in his way; at school he was a sound, healthy boy, good at games, who did his work punctually, and was of blameless character. He made no particular friends; sat through school after school, under various sorts of masters, never inattentive, and never interested. He had a preference for dull and sober teachers, men with whom, as he said, "you knew where you were;" a stimulating teacher bewildered him,—"always talking about poetry and rot." At Cambridge it was the same. He rowed in his College boat; he passed the prescribed examinations; he led a clean healthy decorous life; and no idea, small or great, no sense of beauty, no wonder at the scheme of things, ever entered his head. If by chance he ever found himself in the company of an enthusiastic undergraduate, whose mind and heart were full of burning, incomplete, fantastic thoughts, James listened politely to what he had to say, hazarded no statements, and said, in quiet after-comment, "Gad, how that chap does jaw!" No one ever thought him stupid; he knew what was going on; he was sociable, kind, not the least egotistical, and far too much of a gentleman to exhibit the least complacency in his position or wealth—only he knew exactly what he liked, and had none of the pathetic admiration for talent that is sometimes found in the unintellectual. When he went into the Guards it was just the same. He was popular and respected, friendly with his men, perfectly punctual, capable and respectable. He had no taste for wine or gambling, or disreputable courses. He admired nobody and nothing, and no one obtained the slightest influence over him. At home he was perfectly happy, kind to his sisters, ready to do anything he was asked, and to join in anything that was going on. When he succeeded to the estate, he went quietly to work to find a wife, and married a pretty, contented girl, with the same notions as himself. He never said an unkind thing to her, or to any of his family, and expressed no extravagant affection for any one. He is trustee for all his relations, and always finds time to look after their affairs. He is always ready to subscribe to any good object, and had contrived never to squabble with an angular ritualistic clergyman, who thinks him a devoted son of the Church. He has declined several invitations to stand for Parliament, and has no desire to be elevated to the Peerage. He will probably live to a green old age, and leave an immense fortune. I do not fancy that he is much given to meditate about his latter end; but if he ever lets his mind range over the life beyond the grave, he probably anticipates vaguely that, under somewhat airy conditions, he will continue to enjoy the consideration of his fellow-beings, and deserve their respect.

19

For nearly ten years after we came to Golden End, the parish was administered by an elderly clergyman, who had already been over twenty years in the place. He was little known outside the district at all; I doubt if, between the occasion of his appointment to the living and his death, his name ever appeared in the papers. The Bishop of the diocese knew nothing of him; if the name was mentioned in clerical society, it was dismissed again with some such comment as "Ah, poor Woodward! an able man, I believe, but utterly unpractical;" and yet I have always held this man to be on the whole one of the most remarkable people I have ever known.

Mr. Woodward

He was a tall thin man, with a slight stoop. He could not be called handsome, but his face had a strange dignity and power; he had a pallid complexion, at times indeed like parchment from its bloodlessness, and dark hair which remained dark up to the very end. His eyebrows were habitually drawn up, giving to his face a look of patient endurance; his eyelids drooped over his eyes, which gave his expression a certain appearance of cynicism, but when he opened them full, and turned them upon you, they were dark, passionate, and with a peculiar brightness. His lips were full and large, with beautiful curves, but slightly compressed as a rule, which gave a sense of severity. He was clean shaven, and always very carefully dressed, but in somewhat secular style, with high collars, a frock-coat and waistcoat, a full white cambric tie, and—I shudder to relate it in these days—he was seldom to be seen in black trousers, but wore a shade of dark grey. If you had substituted a black tie for a white one you would have had an ordinary English layman dressed as though for town—for he always wore a tall hat. He often rode about the parish, when he wore a dark grey riding-suit with gaiters. I do not think he ever gave his clothes a thought, but he had the instincts of a fine gentleman, and loved neatness and cleanliness. He had never married, but his house was administered by an elderly sister—rather a grim, majestic personage, with a sharp ironical tongue, and no great indulgence for weakness. Miss Woodward considered herself an invalid, and only appeared in fine weather, driving in a smart little open carriage. They were people of considerable wealth, and the rectory, which was an important house standing in a large glebe, had two gardeners and good stables, and was furnished within, in a dignified way, with old solid furniture. Mr. Woodward had a large library, and at the little dinner-parties that he gave, where the food was of the simplest, the plate was ancient and abundant—old silver candlesticks and salvers in profusion—and a row of family pictures beamed on you from the walls. Mr. Woodward used to say, if any one admired any particular piece of plate, "Yes, I believe it is good; it was all collected by an old uncle of mine, who left it to me with his blessing for my lifetime. Of course I don't quite approve of using it—I believe I ought not even to have two coats—but I can't sell it, and meantime it looks very nice and does no harm." The living was a wealthy one, but it was soon discovered that Mr. Woodward spent all that he received on that head in the parish. He did not pauperise idle parishioners, but he was always ready with a timely gift to tide an honest man over a difficulty. He liked to start the boys in life, and would give a girl a little marriage portion. He paid for a parish nurse, but at the same time he insisted on almsgiving as a duty. "I don't do these things to save you the trouble of giving," he would say, "but to give you a lead; and if I find that the offertories go down, then my subscriptions will go down too;" but he would sometimes say that he feared he was making things difficult for his successor. "I can't help that; if he is a good man the people will understand."

The Church

Mr. Woodward was a great politician and used to say that it was a perpetual temptation to him to sit over the papers in the morning instead of doing his work. But the result was that he always had something to talk about, and his visits were enjoyed by the least spiritual of his parishioners. He was of course eclectic in his politics, and combined a good deal of radicalism with an intense love and veneration for the past. He restored his church with infinite care and taste, and was for ever beautifying it in small ways. He used to say that there were two kinds of church-goers—the people who liked the social aspect of the service, who preferred a blaze of light, hearty singing, and the presence of a large number of people; but that were others who preferred it from the quiet and devotional side, and who were only distracted from the main object of the service by the presence of alert and critical persons. Consequently he had a little transept divided from the body of the church by a simple screen, and kept the lights low within it. The transept was approached by a separate door, and he invited people who could not come for the whole service to slip in for a little of it. At the same time there was plenty of room in the church, and as the parish is not thickly populated, so that you could be sure of finding a seat in any part of the church that suited your mood. He never would have a surpliced choir; and in the morning service, nothing was sung except the canticles and hymns; but there was a fine organ built at his expense, and he offered a sufficiently large salary to secure an organist of considerable taste and skill. He greatly believed in music, and part of the organist's duty was to give a little recital once a week, which was generally well attended. He himself was always present at the choir practices, and the result of the whole was that the congregation sang well, with a tone and a feeling that I have never heard in places where the indigenous materials for choral music were so scanty.

Mr. Woodward talked a good deal on religious subjects, but with an ease and a naturalness which saved his hearers from any feeling of awkwardness or affectation. I have never heard any one who seemed to live so naturally in the seen and the unseen together, and his transitions from mundane to religious talk were made with such simplicity that his hearers felt no embarrassment or pain. After all, the ethical side of life is what we are all interested in—moreover, Mr. Woodward had a decidedly magnetic gift—that gift which, if it had been accompanied with more fire and volubility, would have made him an orator. As it was, the circle to whom he talked felt insensibly interested in what he spoke of, and at the same time there was such a transparent simplicity about the man that no one could have called him affected. His talk it would be impossible to recall; it depended upon all sorts of subtle and delicate effects of personality. Indeed, I remember once after an evening spent in his company, during which he had talked with an extraordinary pathos and emotion, I wrote down what I could remember of it. I look at it now and wonder what the spell was; it seems so ordinary, so simple, so, may I say, platitudinal.

Yet I may mention two or three of his chance sayings. I found him one day in his study deeply engrossed in a book which I saw was the Life of Darwin. He leapt to his feet to greet me, and after the usual courtesies said, "What a wonderful book this is—it is from end to end nothing but a cry for the Nicene Creed! The man walks along, doing his duty so splendidly and nobly, with such single-heartedness and simplicity, and just misses the way all the time; the gospel he wanted is just the other side of the wall. But he must know now, I think. Whenever I go to the Abbey, I always go straight to his grave, and kneel down close beside it, and pray that his eyes may be opened. Very foolish and wrong, I dare say, but I can't help it!"

Another day he found me working at a little pedigree of my father's simple ancestors. I had hunted their names up in an old register, and there was quite a line of simple persons to record. He looked over my shoulder at the sheet while I told him what it was. "Dear old folk!" he said, "I hope you say a prayer now and then for some of them; they belong to you and you to them, but I dare say they were sad Socinians, many of them (laughing). Well, that's all over now. I wonder what they do with themselves over there?"

The Peacock

Mr. Woodward was of course adored by the people of the village. In his trim garden lived a couple of pea-fowl—gruff and selfish birds, but very beautiful to look at. Mr. Woodward had a singular delight in watching the old peacock trail his glories in the sun. They roosted in a tree that overhung the road. There came to stay in the next village a sailor, a ne'er-do-weel, who used to hang about with a gun. One evening Mr. Woodward heard a shot fired in the lane, went out of his study, and found that the sailor had shot the peacock, who was lying on his back in the road, feebly poking out his claws, while the aggressor was pulling the feathers from his tail. Mr. Woodward was extraordinarily moved. The man caught in the act looked confused and bewildered. "Why did you shoot my poor old bird?" said Mr. Woodward. The sailor in apology said he thought it was a pheasant. Mr. Woodward, on the verge of tears, carried the helpless fowl into the garden, but finding it was already dead, interred it with his own hands, told his sister at dinner what had happened, and said no more.

But the story spread, and four stalwart young parishioners of Mr. Woodward's vowed vengeance, caught the luckless sailor in a lane, broke his gun, and put him in the village pond, from which he emerged a lamentable sight, cursing and spluttering; the process was sternly repeated, and not until he handed over all his available cash for the purpose of replacing the bird did his judges desist. Another peacock was bought and presented to Mr. Woodward, the offender being obliged to make the presentation himself with an abject apology, being frankly told that the slightest deviation from the programme would mean another lustral washing.

The above story testifies to the sort of position which Mr. Woodward held in his parish; and what is the most remarkable part of it, indicates the esteem with which he was regarded by the most difficult members of a congregation to conciliate—the young men. But then Mr. Woodward was at ease with the young men. He had talked to them as boys, with a grave politeness which many people hold to be unnecessary in the case of the young. He had encouraged them to come to him in all sorts of little troubles. The men who had resented the loss of Mr. Woodward's peacock knew him as an intimate and honoured family friend; he had tided one over a small money difficulty, and smoothed the path of an ambition for another. He had claimed no sacerdotal rights over the liberties of his people, but such allegiance as he had won was the allegiance that always waits upon sympathy and goodwill; and further, he was shrewd and practical in small concerns, and had the great gift of foreseeing contingencies. He never forgot the clerical character, but he made it unobtrusive, kept it waiting round the corner, and it was always there when it was wanted.

The Professor

I was present once at an interesting conversation between Mr. Woodward and a distinguished university professor who by some accident was staying with myself. The professor had expressed himself as much interested in the conditions of rural life and was lamenting to me the dissidence which he thought was growing up between the clergy and their flocks. I told him about Mr. Woodward and took him to tea. The professor with a courteous frankness attacked Mr. Woodward on the same point. He said that he believed that the raising of theological and clerical standards had had the effect of turning the clergy into a class, enthusiastic, no doubt, but interested in a small circle of things to which they attached extreme importance, though they were mostly traditional or antiquarian. He said that they were losing their hold on English life, and inclined not so much to uphold a scrupulous standard of conduct, as to enforce a preoccupation in doctrinal and liturgical questions, interesting enough, but of no practical importance. Mr. Woodward did not contradict him; the professor, warming to his work, said that the ordinary village sermon was of a futile kind, and possessed no shrewdness or definiteness as a rule. Mr. Woodward asked him to expand the idea—what ought the clergy to preach about? "Well," said the professor, "they ought to touch on politics—not party politics, of course, but social measures, historical developments and so forth. I was present," he went on, "some years ago when, in a country town, the Bishop of the diocese preached a sermon at the parish church, the week after the French had been defeated at Sedan, and the Bishop made not the slightest allusion to the event, though it was the dominant idea in the minds of the sensible members of the congregation; the clergy ought not only to preach politics—they ought to talk politics—they ought to show that they have the same interests as their people."

"Oh, yes," said Mr. Woodward, leaning forward, "I agree with much that you say, Professor—very much; but you look at things in a different perspective. We don't think much about politics here in the country—home politics a little, but foreign politics not at all. When we hear of rumours of war we are not particularly troubled;" (with a smile) "and when I have to try and encourage an old bedridden woman who is very much bewildered with this world, and has no imagination left to deal with the next—and who is sadly afraid of her long journey in the dark—when I have to try and argue with a naughty boy who has got some poor girl into trouble, and doesn't feel in his heart that he has done a selfish or a brutal thing, am I to talk to them about the battle of Sedan, or even about the reform of the House of Lords?"

The professor smiled grimly, but perhaps a little foolishly, and did not take up the challenge. But Mr. Woodward said to me a few days afterwards: "I was very much interested in your friend the professor—a most amiable, and, I should think, unselfish person. How good of him to interest himself in the parish clergy! But you know, my dear boy, the intellectual atmosphere is a difficult one to live in—a man needs some very human trial of his own to keep him humble and sane. I expect the professor wants a long illness!" (smiling) "No, I dare say he is very good in his own place, and does good work for Christ, but he is a man clothed in soft raiment in these wilds, and you and I must do all we can to prevent him from rewriting the Lord's Prayer. I am afraid he thinks there is a sad absence of the intellectual element in it. It must be very distressing to him to think how often it is used; and yet there is not an allusion to politics in it—not even to comprehensive measures of social reform."

Mr. Woodward's Sermons
Mr. Woodward's sermons were always a pleasure to me. He told me once that he had a great dislike to using conventional religious language; and thus, though he was in belief something of a High Churchman, he was so careful to avoid catch-words or party formulas that few people suspected how high the doctrine was. I took an elderly evangelical aunt to church once, when Mr. Woodward preached a sermon on baptismal regeneration of rather an advanced type. I shuddered to think of the denunciations which I anticipated after church; indeed, I should not have been surprised if my aunt had gathered up her books—she was a masculine personage—and swept out of the building. Both on the contrary, she listened intently, rather moist-eyed, I thought, to the discourse, and afterwards spoke to me with extreme emphasis of it as a real gospel sermon. Mr. Woodward wrote his sermons, but often I think departed from the text. He discoursed with a simple tranquillity of manner that made each hearer feel as if he was alone with him. His allusions to local events were thrilling in their directness and pathos; and in passing, I may say that he was the only man I ever heard who made the giving out of notices, both in manner and matter, into a fine art. On Christmas Day he used to speak about the events of the year; one winter there was a bad epidemic of diphtheria in the village, and several children died. The shepherd on one of the farms, a somewhat gruff and unsociable character, lost two little children on Christmas Eve. Mr. Woodward, unknown to me at the time, had spent the evening with the unhappy man, who was almost beside himself with grief.

The Christmas Sermon

In the sermon he began quite simply, describing the scene of the first Christmas Eve in a few picturesque words. Then he quoted Christina Rossetti's Christmas Carol—

"In the bleak mid-winter
Wintry winds made moan,"
dwelling on the exquisite words in a way which brought the tears to my eyes. When he came to the lines describing the gifts made to Christ—

"If I were a shepherd
I would bring a lamb,"
he stopped dead for some seconds. I feel sure that he had not thought of the application before. Then he looked down the church and said—

"I spent a long time yesterday in the house of one who follows the calling of a shepherd among us.... He has given two lambs to Christ."

There was an uncontrollable throb of emotion in the large congregation, and I confess that the tears filled my eyes. Mr. Woodward went on—

"Yes, it has pleased God to lead him through deep waters; but I do not think that he will altogether withhold from him something of his Christmas joy. He knows that they are safe with Christ—safe with Christ, and waiting for him there—and that will be more and more of a joy, and less and less of a sorrow as the years go on, till God restores him the dear children He has taken from him now. We must not forget him in our prayers."

Then after a pause he resumed. There was no rhetoric or oratory about it; but I have never in my life heard anything so absolutely affecting and moving—any word which seemed to go so straight from heart to heart; it was the genius of humanity.

A few months after this Mr. Woodward died, as he always wished to die, quite suddenly, in his chair. He had often said to me that he did hope he wouldn't die in bed, with bed-clothes tucked under his chin, and medicine bottles by him; he said he was sure he would not make an edifying end under the circumstances. His heart had long been weak; and he was found sitting with his head on his breast as though asleep, smiling to himself. In one hand his pen was still clasped. I have never seen such heartfelt grief as was shown at his funeral. His sister did not survive him a month. The week after her death I walked up to the rectory, and found the house being dismantled. Mr. Woodward's books were being packed into deal cases; the study was already a dusty, awkward room. It was strange to think of the sudden break-up of that centre of beautiful life and high example. All over and done! Yet not all; there are many grateful hearts who do not forget Mr. Woodward; and what he would have thought and what he would have said are still the natural guide for conduct in a dozen simple households. If death must come, it was so that he would have wished it; and Mr. Woodward could be called happy in life and death perhaps more than any other man I have known.

20
Mr. Cuthbert

Who was to be Mr. Woodward's successor? For some weeks we had lived in a state of agitated expectancy. One morning, soon after breakfast, a card was brought to me—The Rev. Cyril Cuthbert. I went down to the drawing-room and found my mother talking to a young clergyman, who rose at my entrance, and informed me that he had been offered the living, and that he had ventured to call and consult me, adding that he had been told I was all-powerful in the parish. I was distinctly prepossessed by his appearance, and perhaps by his appreciation, however exaggerated, of my influence; he was a small man with thin features, but bronzed and active; his hair was parted in the middle and lay in wiry waves on each side. He had small, almost feminine, hands and feet, and rather a delicate walk. He was entirely self-possessed, very genial in talk, with a pleasant laugh; at the same time he gave me an impression of strength. He was dressed in very old and shabby clothes, of decidedly clerical cut, but his hat and coat were almost green from exposure to weather. Yet he was obviously a gentleman. I gathered that he was the son of a country squire, that he had been at a public school and Oxford, and that he had been for some years a curate in a large manufacturing town. As we talked my impressions became more definite; the muscles of the jaw were strongly developed, and I began to fancy that the genial manner concealed a considerable amount of self-will. He had the eye which I have been led to associate with the fanatic, of a certain cold blue, shallow and impenetrable, which does not let you far into the soul, but meets you with a bright and unshrinking gaze.

At his request I accompanied him to church and vicarage. At the latter, he said to me frankly that he was a poor man, and that he would not be able to keep it up in the same style—"Indeed," he said with a smile, "I don't think it would be right to do so." I said that I didn't think it very material, but that as a matter of fact I thought that the perfection of Mr. Woodward's arrangements had had a humanising influence in the place. At the church he was pleased at the neatness and general air of use that the building had; but he looked with disfavour at the simple arrangements of the chancel. I noticed that he bowed and murmured a few words of prayer when he entered the building. When we had examined the church he said to me, "To speak frankly, Mr. ——,—I don't know what your views are,—but what is the church tone of this place like?" I said that I hardly knew how to describe it—the church certainly played a large part in the lives of the parishioners; but that I supposed that Mr. Woodward would perhaps be called old-fashioned. "Yes, indeed," sighed Mr. Cuthbert, looking wearily round and shrugging his shoulders. "The altar indeed is distinctly dishonouring to the Blessed Sacrament—no attempt at Catholic practice or tradition. There is not, I see, even a second altar in the church; but, please God, if He sends me here we will change all that."

Before we left the church he fell on his knees and prayed with absolute self-absorption.

When we got outside he said to me: "May I tell you something? I have just returned from a visit to a friend of mine, a priest at A——; he has got everything—simply everything; he is a noble fellow—if I could but hope to imitate him."

A—— was, I knew, a great railway depôt, and thinking that Mr. Cuthbert did not fully understand how very rural a parish we were, I said, "I am afraid there is not very much scope here for great activity. We have a reading-room and a club, but it has never been a great success—the people won't turn out in the evenings."

"Reading-rooms and clubs," said Mr. Cuthbert in high disdain; "I did not mean that kind of thing at all—I was thinking of things much nearer the heart of the people. Herries has incense and lights, the eucharistic vestments, he reserves the sacrament—you may see a dozen people kneeling before the tabernacle whenever you enter the church—he has often said to me that he doesn't know how he could keep hope alive in his heart in the midst of such vice and sin, if it were not for the thought of the Blessed Presence, in the midst of it, in the quiet church. He has a sisterhood in his parish too under a very strict rule. They never leave the convent, and spend whole days in intercession. The sacrament has been reserved there for fifteen years. Then confession is urged plainly upon all, and it is a sight to make one thrill with joy to see the great rough navvies bending before Herries as he sits in his embroidered stole, they telling him the secrets of their hearts, and he bringing them nearer to the joy of their Lord. Some of the workmen in the parish are the most frequent at confession. Oh! he is a noble fellow; he tells me he has no time for visiting—positively no time at all. His whole day is spent in deepening the devotional life—the hours are recited in the church—he gives up ten hours every week to the direction of penitents, and he must spend, I should say, two hours a day at his priedieu. He says he could not have strength for his work if he did not. His sermons are beautiful; he speaks from the heart without preparation. He says he has learnt to trust the Spirit, and just says what is given him to say.

"Then he is devoted to his choristers, and they to him; it is a privilege to see him surrounded by them in their little cassocks while he leads them in a simple meditation. And he is a man of a deeply tender spirit—I have seen him, dining with his curates, burst into tears at the mere mention of the name of the dear Mother of Christ. I ought not to trouble you with all this—I am too enthusiastic! But the sight of him has put it into my heart more than anything else I have ever known to try and build up a really Catholic centre, which might do something to leaven the heavy Protestantism which is the curse of England. One more thing which especially struck me; it moved me to tears to hear one of his great rough fellows—a shunter, I believe, who is often overthrown by the demon of strong drink—talk so simply and faithfully of the Holy Mass: what rich associations that word has! Nothing but eternity will ever reveal the terrible loss which the disuse of that splendid word has inflicted on our unhappy England."

I was too much bewildered by this statement to make any adequate reply, but said to console him that I thought the parish was wonderfully good, and prepared to look upon the clergyman as a friend. "Yes," said Mr. Cuthbert, "that is all very well for a beginning, but it must be something more than that. They must revere him as steward of the mysteries of God—they must be ready to open their inmost heart to him; they must come to recognise that it is through him, as a consecrated priest of Christ, that the highest spiritual blessings can reach them: that he alone can confer upon them the absolution which can set them free from the guilt of sin."

I felt that I ought not to let Mr. Cuthbert think that I was altogether of the same mind with him in these matters and so I said: "Well, you must remember that all this is unfamiliar here; Mr. Woodward did not approve of confession—he held that habitual confession was weakening to the moral nature, and encouraged the most hysterical kind of egotism—though no one was more ready to listen to any one's troubles and to give the most loving advice in real difficulties. But as to the point about absolution, I think he felt, and I should agree with him, that God only can forgive sin, and that the clergy are merely the human interpreters of that forgiveness; it is so much more easy to apprehend a great moral principle like the forgiveness of sin from another human being than to arrive at it in the silence of one's own troubled heart."

Mr. Cuthbert smiled, not very pleasantly, and said, "I had hoped you would have shared my views more warmly—it is a disappointment! seriously, the power to bind and loose conferred on the Apostles by Christ Himself—does that mean nothing?"

"Yes, indeed," I said, "the clergy are the accredited ministers in the matter, of course, and they have a sacred charge, but as to powers conferred upon the Apostles, it seems that other powers were conferred on His followers which they no longer possess—they were to drink poison with impunity, handle venomous snakes, and even to heal the sick."

"Purely local and temporary provisions," said Mr. Cuthbert, "which we have no doubt forfeited—if indeed we have forfeited them—by want of faith. The other was a gift for time and eternity."

"I don't remember," I said, "that any such distinction was laid down in the Gospel—but in any case you would not maintain, would you, that they possessed the power proprio motu? To push it to extremes, that if a man was absolved by a priest, God's forgiveness was bound to follow, even if the priest were deceived as to the reality of the penitence which claimed forgiveness."

Mr. Cuthbert frowned and said, "To me it is not a question of theorising. It is a purely practical matter. I look upon it in this way—if a man is absolved by a priest, he is sure he is forgiven; if he is not, he cannot be sure of forgiveness."

"I should hold," I said, "that it was purely a matter of inner penitence. But I did not mean to entangle you in a theological argument—and I hope we are at one on essential matters."

As we walked back I pointed out to him some of my favourite views—the long back of the distant downs; the dark forest tract that closed the northern horizon—but he looked with courteous indifference: his heart was full of Catholic tradition.

We heard a few days after that he had accepted the living, and we asked him to come and stay with us while he was getting into the vicarage, which he was furnishing with austere severity. Mr. Woodward's pleasant dark study became a somewhat grim library, with books in deal shelves, carpeted with matting and with a large deal table to work at. Mr. Cuthbert dwelt much on the thought of sitting there in a cassock with a tippet, but I do not think he had any of the instincts of a student—it was rather the mise-en-scène that pleased him. A bedroom became an oratory, with a large ivory crucifix. The dining-room he called his refectory, and he had a scheme at one time of having two young men to do the housework and cooking, which fortunately fell through, though they were to have had cassocks with cord-girdles, and to have been called lay brothers. On the other hand he was a very pleasant visitor, as long as theological discussions were avoided. He was bright, gay, outwardly sympathetic, full of a certain kind of humour, and with all the ways of a fine gentleman. The more I disagreed with him the more I liked him personally.

One evening after dinner, as we sat smoking—he was a great smoker—we had a rather serious discussion. I said to him that I really should like to understand what his theory of church work was.

Catholic Tradition
"It is all summed up in two phrases," said Mr. Cuthbert. "Catholic practice—Catholic tradition. I hold that the Reformation inflicted a grievous blow upon this country. To break with Rome was almost inevitable, I admit, because of the corruption of doctrine that was beginning; but we need not have thrown over all manner of high and holy ways and traditions, solemn accessories of worship, tender assistances to devotion, any more than the Puritans were bound to break statues and damage stained glass windows."

"Quite so," I said; "but where does this Catholic tradition come from?"

"From the Primitive Church," said Mr. Cuthbert. "As far back as we can trace the history of church practice we find these, or many of these, exquisite ceremonies, which I for one think it a solemn duty to try and restore."

"But after all," I said, "they are of human origin, are they not? You would not say that they have a divine sanction?"

"Well," said Mr. Cuthbert, "their sanction is practically divine. We read that in the last days spent by our Lord in His glorified nature on the earth, He 'spake to them of the things concerning the Kingdom of God.' I myself think it is only reasonable to suppose that He was laying down the precise ceremonial that He wished should attend the worship of His Kingdom. I do not think that extravagant."

"But," I said, "was not the whole tenor of His teaching against such ceremonial precision? Did He not for His Sacraments choose the simplest and humblest actions of daily life—eating and drinking? Was He not always finding fault with the Pharisees for forgetting spiritual truth in their zeal for tradition and practice?"

"Yes," said Mr. Cuthbert, "for forgetting the weightier matters of the law; but He approved of their ceremonial. He said: 'These ought ye to have done, and not to have left the other undone.'"

"I believe myself," I said, "that He felt they should have obeyed their conscience in the matter; but surely the whole of the teaching of the Gospel is to loose human beings from tyranny of detail, and to teach them to live a simple life on great principles?"

"I cannot agree," said Mr. Cuthbert. "The instinct for reverence, for the reverent and seemly expression of spiritual feeling, for the symbolic representation of spiritual feeling, for the symbolic representation of divine truths is a depreciated one, but a true one; and this instinct He graciously defined, fortified, and consecrated; and I believe that the Church was following the true guidance of the Spirit in the matter, when it slowly built up the grand and massive fabric of Catholic practice and tradition."

"But," I said, "who are the Church? There are a great many people who feel the exact opposite of what you maintain—and true Christians too."

"They are grievously mistaken," said Mr. Cuthbert, "and suffer an irreparable loss."

"But who is to decide?" I said, a little nettled.

"A General Œcumenical Council would be competent to do so," said Mr. Cuthbert.

"Do you mean of the Anglican Communion?" I said.

"Oh dear, no," said Mr. Cuthbert. "The Anglican Communion indeed! No; such a Council must have representatives of all Churches who have received and maintain the Divine succession."

"But," said I, "you must know that the thing is impossible. Who could summon such a Council, and who would attend it?"

"That is not my business," said Mr. Cuthbert; "I do not want any such Council. I am sure of my position; it is only you and others who wish to sacrifice the most exquisite part of Christian life who need such a solution. I am content with what I know; and humbly and faithfully I shall attempt as far as I can to follow the dictates of my conscience in the matter to endeavor to bring it home to the consciences of my flock."

I felt I could not carry the argument further without loss of temper; but it was surprising to me how I continued to like, and even to respect, the man.

He has not, it must be confessed, obtained any great hold on the parish. Mr. Woodward's quiet, delicate, fatherly work has gone; but Mr. Cuthbert has a few women who attend confession, and he is content. He has adorned the church according to his views, and the congregation think it rather pretty. They do not dislike his sermons, though they do not understand them; and as for his vestments, they regard them with a mild and somewhat bewildered interest. They like to see Mr. Cuthbert, he is so pleasant and good-humoured. He is assiduous in his visiting, and very assiduous in holding daily services, which are entirely unattended. He has no priestly influence; and I fear it would pain him deeply if he knew that his social influence is considerable. Personally, I find him a pleasant neighbour and highly congenial companion. We have many agreeable talks; and when I am in that irritable tense mood which is apt to develop in solitude, and which can only be cleared by an ebullition of spleen, I walk up to the vicarage and have a theological argument. It does neither myself nor Mr. Cuthbert any harm, and we are better friends than ever—indeed, he calls me quite the most agreeable Erastian he knows.

21
The Recluse
Let me try to sketch the most Arcadian scholar I have ever seen or dreamed of; they are common enough in books; the gentleman of high family, with lustrous eyes and thin veined hands, who sits among musty folios—Heaven knows what he is supposed to be studying, or why they need be musty—who is in some very nebulous way believed to watch the movements of the heavens, who takes no notice of his prattling golden-

haired daughter, except to print an absent kiss upon her brow—if there are such persons they are hard to encounter.

There is a little market-town a mile or two away, nestled among steep valleys; the cows that graze on the steep fields that surround it look down into the chimney-pots and back gardens. One of the converging valleys is rich in woods, and has a pleasant trout-stream, that flows among elders, bickers along by woodland corners, and runs brimming through rich water meadows, full of meadowsweet and willow-herb—the place in summer has a hot honied smell. You need not follow the road, but you may take an aimless footpath, which meanders from stile to stile in a leisurely way. After a mile or so a little stream bubbles in on the left; and close beside it an old deep farm-road, full of boulders and mud in winter, half road, half water-course, plunges down from the wood. All the hedges are full of gnarled roots fringed with luxuriant ferns. On a cloudy summer day it is like a hothouse here, and the flowers know it and revel in the warm growing air. Higher and higher the road goes; then it passes a farm-house, once an ancient manor: the walls green with lichen and moss, and a curious ancient cognizance, a bear with a ragged staff clasped in his paws, over the doorway. The farm is embowered in huge sprawling laurels and has a little garden, with box hedges and sharp savoury smells of herbs and sweet-william, and a row of humming hives. Push open the byre gate and go further yet; we are near the crest of the hill now: just below the top grows a thick wood of larches, set close together. You would not know there was a house in here. There is a little rustic gate at the corner of the plantation, and a path, just a track, rarely trodden, soft with a carpet of innumerable larch-needles.

Presently you come in sight of a small yellow stone house; not a venerable house, nor a beautiful one—if anything, a little pretentious, and looking as if the heart of the plantation had been cut out to build it as indeed it was; round-topped windows, high parapets, no roof visible, and only one rather makeshift chimney; the whole air of it rather sinister, and at the same time shamefaced—a little as though it set out to be castellated and had suddenly shrunk and collapsed, and been hastily finished. A gravel walk very full of weeds runs immediately round the house; there is no garden, but a small enclosure for cabbages grown very rank. In most of the windows hang dirty-looking blinds half pulled down; a general air of sordid neglect broods over the place. Here in this house had lived for many years—and, for all I know, lives there still—a retired gentleman, a public school and University man, who had taken high honours at the latter; not rich, but with a competence. What had caused his seclusion from the world I do not know, and I am not particular to inquire; whether a false step and the forced abandonment of a career, a disappointment of some kind, a hypochondriacal whim, or a settled and deliberate resolution. I know not, but always hoped the last.

From some slight indications I have thought that, for some reason or other, in youth, my recluse had cause to think that his life would not be a long one—his selection of a site was apparently fortuitous. He preferred a mild climate, and, it seems, took a fancy to the very remote and sequestered character of the valley; he bought a few acres of land, planted them with larches, and in the centre erected the unsightly house which I have described.

Inside the place was rather more attractive than you would have expected. There was a pinched little entry, rather bare, and a steep staircase leading to the upper regions; in front of you a door leading to some offices; on the left a door that opened into a large room to which all the rest of the house had been sacrificed. It had three windows, much overshadowed by the larches, which indeed at one corner actually touched the house and swept the windows as they swayed in the breeze. The room was barely furnished, with a carpet faded beyond recognition, and high presses, mostly containing books. An oak table stood near one of the windows, where our hermit took his meals; another table, covered with books, was set near the fireplace; at the far end a door led into an ugly slit of a room lighted by a skylight, where he slept. But I gathered that for days together he did not go to bed, but dozed in his chair. On the walls hung two or three portraits, black with age. One of an officer in a military uniform of the last century with a huge, adumbrating cocked-hat; a divine in bands and wig; and a pinched-looking lady in blue silk with two boys. His only servant was an elderly strong-looking woman of about fifty, with a look of intense mental suffering on her face, and weary eyes which she seldom lifted from the floor. I never heard her utter more than three consecutive words. She was afflicted I heard, not from herself, with a power of seeing apparitions, not, curiously, in the house, but in the wood all round; she told Mr. Woodward that "the dead used to look in at the window at noon and beckon her out." In consequence of this she had not set foot outside the doors for twenty years, except once, when her master had been attacked by sudden illness. The only outside servant he had was a surly man who lived in a cottage a quarter of a mile away on the high-road, who marketed for them, drew water, and met the carrier's cart which brought their necessaries.

The man himself was a student of history: he never wrote, except a few marginal notes in his books. He was totally ignorant of what was going on, took in no papers, and asked no questions as to current events. He received no letters, and the only parcels that came to him were boxes of books from a

London library—memoirs, historical treatises, and biographies of the last century. I take it he had a minute knowledge of the social and political life of England up to the beginning of the present century; he received no one but Mr. Woodward who saw him two or three times a year, and it was with Mr. Woodward that I went, making the excuse (which was actually the case) that some literary work that I was doing was suspended for want of books.

We were shown in; he did not rise to receive us, but greeted us with extreme cordiality, and an old-fashioned kind of courtesy, absolutely without embarrassment. He was a tall, thin man, with a fair complexion, and straggling hair and beard. He seemed to be in excellent health; and I learnt that in the matter of food and drink he was singularly abstemious, which accounted for his clear complexion and brilliant eye. He smoked in moderation a very fragrant tobacco of which he gave me a small quantity, but refused to say where he obtained it. There was an air of infinite contentment about him. He seemed to me to hope for nothing and expect nothing from life; to live in the moment and for the moment. If ever I saw serene happiness written on a face in legible characters, it was there. He talked a little on theological points, with an air of gentle good-humour, to Mr. Woodward, somewhat as you might talk to a child, with amiable interest in the unexpected cleverness of its replies; he gave me the information I requested clearly and concisely but with no apparent zest, and seemed to have no wish to dwell on the subject or to part with his store of knowledge.

His one form of exercise was long vague walks; in the winter he rarely left the house except on moonlight nights; but in the summer he was accustomed to start as soon as it was light, and to ramble, never on the roads, but by unfrequented field-paths, for miles and miles, generally returning before the ordinary world was astir. On hot days he would sit by the stream in a very remote nook beneath a high bank where the water ran swiftly down a narrow channel, and swung into a deep black pool; here, I was told, he would stay for hours with his eyes fixed on the water, lost in some mysterious reverie. I take it he was a poet without power of expression, and his heart was as clean as a child's.

Modern Life
It is the fashion now to talk with much affected weariness of the hurry and bustle of modern life. No doubt such things are to be found if you go in search of them; and to have your life attended by a great quantity of either is generally held to be a sign of success. But the truth is, that this is what ordinary people like. The ordinary man has no precise idea what to do with his time. He needs to have it filled up by a good many conflicting and petty duties, and if it is filled he has a feeling that he is useful. But many of these

duties are only necessary because of the existence of each other; it is a vicious circle. "What are those fields for?" said a squire who had lately succeeded to an estate, as he walked round with the bailiff. "To grow oats, sir." "And what do you do with the oats?" "Feed the horses, sir." "And what do you want the horses for?" "To plough the fields, sir." That is what much of the bustle of modern life consists of.

Solitude and silence are a great strain; but if you enjoy them they are at least harmless, which is more than can be said of many activities. Such is not perhaps the temper in which continents are explored, battles won, empires extended, fortunes made. But whatever concrete gain we make for ourselves must be taken from others; and we ought to be very certain indeed of the meaning of this life, and the nature of the world to which we all migrate, before we immerse ourselves in self-contrived businesses. To be natural, to find our true life, to be independent of luxuries, not to be at the mercy of prejudices and false ideals—that is the secret of life: who can say that it is a secret that we most of us make our own? My recluse, I think, was nearer the Kingdom of Heaven, where places are not laid according to the table of precedence, than many men who have had biographies and statues, and who will be, I fear, sadly adrift in the world of silence into which they may be flung.

22
Nov. 6, 1890.

To-day the gale had blown itself out; all yesterday it blustered round corners, shook casements, thundered in the chimneys, and roared in the pines. Now it is bright and fresh, and the steady wind is routing one by one the few clouds that hang in the sky. I came in yesterday at dusk, and the whole heaven was full of great ragged, lowering storm-wreaths, weeping wildly and sadly; now the rain is over, though in the morning a sudden dash of great drops mingled with hail made the windows patter; but the sun shone out very low and white from the clouds, even while the hail leapt on the window-sill.

I took the field-path that wanders aimlessly away below the house; the water lay in the grass, and the sodden leaves had a bitter smell. The copses were very bare, and the stream ran hoarse and turbid. The way wound by fallows and hedges—now threading a steep copse, now along the silent water-meadows, now through an open forest space, with faggots tied and piled, or by a cattle byre. Here and there I turned into a country lane, till at last the village of Spyfield lay before me, with the ancient church of dark sandstone and the little street of handsome Georgian houses, very neat and prim—a place, you would think, where every one went to bed at ten, and where no murmurs of wars ever penetrated.

Just beyond the village, my friend, Mr. Campden, the great artist, has built himself a palace. It is somewhat rococo, no doubt, with its marble terrace and its gilded cupolas. But it gleams in the dark hanging wood with an exotic beauty of its own, as if a Genie had uprooted it from a Tuscan slope, and planted it swiftly, in an unfamiliar world, in an hour of breathless labour between the twilight and the dawn. Still, fantastic as it is, it is an agreeable contrast to the brick-built mansions, with their slated turrets, that have lately, alas, begun to alight in our woodlands.

Mr. Campden
Mr. Campden is a real prince, a Lorenzo the Magnificent; not only is he the painter of pictures which command a high price, though to me they are little more than harmonious wallpaper; but he binds books, makes furniture, weaves tapestry, and even bakes tiles and pottery; and the slender minaret that rises from a plain, windowless building on the right, is nothing but a concealed chimney. Moreover, he inherited through a relative's death an immense fortune, so that he is a millionaire as well. To-day I followed the little steep lane that skirts his domain, and halted for a moment at a great grille of ironwork, which gives the passer-by a romantic and generous glimpse of a pleached alley, terminated by a mysterious leaden statue. I peeped in cautiously, and saw the great man in a blue suit, with a fur cloak thrown round his shoulders, a slouched hat set back from his forehead, and a loose red tie gleaming from his low-cut collar. I was near enough to see his wavy white hair and beard, his keen eyes, his thin hands, as he paced delicately about, breathing the air, and looking critically at the exquisite house beyond him. I am sure of a welcome from Mr. Campden—indeed, he has a princely welcome for all the world—but to-day I felt a certain simple schoolboy shyness, which ill accords with Mr. Campden's Venetian manner. It is delightful after long rusticity to be with him, but it is like taking a part in some solemn and affected dance; to Mr. Campden I am the student-recluse, and to be gracefully bantered accordingly, and asked a series of questions on matters with which I am wholly unacquainted, but which are all part of the setting with which his pictorial mind has dowered me. On my first visit to him I spoke of the field-names of the neighbourhood, and so Mr. Campden speaks to me of Domesday Book, which I have never seen. I happened to express—in sheer wantonness—an interest in strange birds, and I have ever since to Mr. Campden been a man who, in the intervals of reading Domesday Book, stands in all weathers on hilltops, or by reedy stream-ends,

watching for eagles and swans, like a Roman augur—indeed Augur is the name he gives me—our dear Augur—when I am introduced to his great friends.

Mr. Campden has an infinite contempt for the gentlemen of the neighbourhood, whom he treats with splendid courtesy, and the kind of patronising amusement with which one listens to the prattle of a rustic child. It is a matter of unceasing merriment to me to see him with a young squire of the neighbourhood, an intelligent young fellow who has travelled a good deal, and is a considerable reader. He has a certain superficial shyness, and consequently has never been able to secure enough of the talk for himself to show Mr. Campden what he is thinking of; and Mr. Campden at once boards him with questions about the price of eggs and the rotation of crops, calling him, "Will Honeycomb" from the Spectator; and when plied with nervous questions as to Perugino or Carlo Dolce, saying grandiloquently, "My dear young man, I know nothing whatever about it; I leave that to the critics. I am a republican in art, a red indeed, ha, ha! And you and I must not concern ourselves with such things. Here we are in the country, and we must talk of bullocks. Tell me now, in Lorton market last week, what price did a Tegg fetch?"

Mr. Campden is extraordinarily ignorant of all country matters, and has a small stock of ancient provincial words, not indigenous to the neighbourhood, but gathered from local histories, that he produces with complacent pride. Indeed, I do not know that I ever saw a more ludicrous scene than Mr. Campden talking agriculture to a distinguished scientific man, whom a neighbouring squire had brought over to tea with him, and whom he took for a landowner. To hear Mr. Campden explaining a subject with which he was not acquainted to a courteous scientist, who did not even know to what he was alluding, was a sight to make angels laugh.

But to-day I let Mr. Campden pace like a peacock up and down his pleasaunces, with his greyhound following him, and threaded the water-meadows homewards. I gave myself up to the luxurious influences of solitude and cool airs, and walked slowly, indifferent where I went, by sandstone pits, by brimming streams, through dripping coverts, till the day declined. What did I think of? I hardly dare confess. There are two or three ludicrous, pitiful ambitions that lurk in the corners of my mind, which, when I am alone and aimless, I take out and hold, as a child holds a doll, while fancy invests them with radiant hues. These and no other were my mental pabulum. I know they cannot be realised—indeed, I do not desire them—but these odd and dusty fancies remain with me from far-off boyish days; and many a time have I thus paraded them in all their silliness.

Home

But the hedgerow grasses grew indistinguishably grey; the cattle splashed home along the road; the sharp smell of wood smoke from cottage fires, piled for the long evenings, stole down the woodways; pheasants muttered and crowed in the coverts, and sprang clanging to their roosts. The murmur of the stream became louder and more insistent; and as I turned the corner of the wood, it was with a glow of pleasure that I saw the sober gables of Golden End, and the hall window, like a red solemn eye, gaze cheerily upon the misty valley.

23
July 7, 1891.

In the Woods

I cannot tell why it is, but to be alone among woods, especially towards evening, is often attended with a vague unrest, an unsubstantial awe, which, though of the nature of pleasure, is perilously near the confines of horror. On certain days, when the nerves are very alert and the woods unusually still, I have known the sense become almost insupportable. There is a certain feeling of being haunted, followed, watched, almost dogged, which is bewildering and unmanning. Foolish as it may appear, I have found the carrying of a gun almost a relief on such occasions. But what heightens the sense in a strange degree is the presence of still water. A stream is lively—it encourages and consoles; but the sight of a long dark lake, with the woods coming down to the water's edge, is a sight so solemn as to be positively oppressive. Each kind of natural scenery has its own awe—the genius loci, so to speak. On a grassy down there is the terror of the huge open-eyed gaze of the sky. In craggy mountains there is something wild and beastlike frowning from the rocks. Among ice and snow there is something mercilessly pure and averse to life; but neither of these is so intense or definite as the horror of still woods and silent waters. The feeling is admirably expressed by Mr. George Macdonald in Phantastes, a magical book. It is that sensation of haunting presences hiding behind trees, watching us timidly from the fern, peeping from dark copses, resting among fantastic and weather-worn rocks, that finds expression in the stories of Dryads and fairies, which seem so deeply implanted in the mind of man. Who, on coming out through dark woods into some green sequestered lawn, set deep in the fringing forest, has not had the sensation of an interrupted revel, as festivity suddenly abandoned by wild, ethereal natures, who have shrunk in silent alarm back into the sheltering shades? If only one had been more wary, and stolen a moment earlier upon the unsuspecting company!

But there is a darker and cloudier sensation, the admonitus locorum, which I have experienced upon fields of battle, and places where some huge tragedy of human suffering and excitement has been wrought. I have felt it upon the rustic ploughland of Jena, and on the grassy slopes of Flodden; it has crept over me under the mouldering walls and frowning gateways of old guarded towns; and not only there, where it may be nothing but the reflex of shadowy imaginations, but on wind-swept moors and tranquil valleys, I have felt, by some secret intuition, some overpowering tremor of spirit, that here some desperate strife has been waged, some primeval conflict enacted. There is a spot in the valley of Llanthony, a grassy tumulus among steep green hills, where the sense came over me with an uncontrollable throb of insight, that here some desperate stand was made, some barbarous Themopylæ lost or won.

A Dark Secret

There is a place near Golden End where I encountered a singular experience. I own that I never pass it now without some obsession of feeling; indeed, I will confess that when I am alone I take a considerable circuit to avoid the place. An ancient footway, trodden deep in a sandy covert, winds up through a copse, and comes out into a quiet place far from the high-road, in the heart of the wood. Here stands a mouldering barn, and there are two or three shrubs, an escalonia and a cypress, that testify to some remote human occupation. There is a stretch of green sward, varied with bracken, and on the left a deep excavation, where sand has been dug: in winter, a pool; in summer, a marshy place full of stiff, lush water-plants. In this place, time after time as I passed it, there seemed to be a strange silence. No bird seemed to sing here, no woodland beast to frisk here; a secret shame or horror rested on the spot. It was with no sense of surprise, but rather of resolved doubt, that I found, one bright morning, two labouring men bent over some object that lay upon the ground. When they saw me, they seemed at first to hesitate, and then asked me to come and look. It was a spectacle of singular horror: they had drawn from the marshy edge of the pool the tiny skeleton of a child, wrapped in some oozy and ragged cloths; the slime dripping from the eyeless cavities of the little skull, and the weeds trailing over the unsightly cerements. It had caught the eye of one of them as they were passing. "The place has always had an evil name," said one of them with a strange solemnity. There had been a house there, I gathered, inhabited by a mysterious evil family, a place of dark sin and hideous tradition. The stock had dwindled down to a wild solitary woman, who extracted a bare sustenance out of a tiny farm, and who alternated long periods of torpid gloom with disgusting orgies of drunkenness. Thirty years ago she had died, and the farm had remained so long unlet that it was at last pulled down, and the land planted with wood. Subsequent investigations revealed nothing; and the body had lain there, it was thought, for fully that time, preserved from decay by an iron-bound box in which it had been enclosed, and of which some traces still remained in reddish smears of rust and clotted nails. That picture—the sunlit morning, the troubled faces of the men, the silent spectatorial woods—has dwelt with me ineffaceably.

Obsession
Again, I have been constantly visited by the same inexplicable sensation in a certain room at Golden End. The room in question is a great bare chamber at the top of the house: the walls are plastered, and covered in all directions by solid warped beams; through the closed and dusty window the sunlight filters sordidly into the room. I do not know why it has never been furnished, but I gathered that my father took an unexplained dislike to the room from the first. The odd feature of it is, that in the wall at one end is a small door, as of a cupboard, some feet from the ground, which opens, not as you would expect into a cupboard, but into a loft, where you can see the tiles, the brickwork of the clustered chimney-stacks, and the plastered lathwork of the floor, in and below the joists of the timber. This strange opening can never have been a window, because the shutter is of the same date as the house; still less a door, for it is hardly possible to squeeze through it; but as the loft into which it looks is an accretion of later date than the room itself, it seems to me that the garret may have been once a granary up to which sacks were swung from the ground by a pulley; and this is made more possible by the existence of some iron staples on the outer side of it, that appear to have once controlled some simple mechanism.

The Evil Room
The room is now a mere receptacle for lumber, but it is strange that all who enter it, even the newest inmate of the house, take an unaccountable dislike to the place. I have myself struggled against the feeling; I once indeed shut myself up there on a sunny afternoon, and endeavoured to shame myself by pure reason out of the disagreeable, almost physical sensation that at once came over me, but all in vain; there was something about the bare room, with its dusty and worm-eaten floor, the hot stagnant air, the floating motes in the stained sunlight, and above all the sinister little door, that gave me a discomfort that it seems impossible to express in speech. My own room must have been the scene of many a serious human event. Sick men must have lain there; hopeless prayers must have echoed there; children must have been born there, and souls must have quitted their shattered tenement beneath its ancient panels. But these have after all been normal

experiences; in the other room, I make no doubt, some altogether abnormal event must have happened, something of which the ethereal aroma, as of some evil, penetrating acid, must have bitten deep into wall and floor, and soaked the very beam of the roof with anxious and disturbed oppression. In feverish fancy I see strange things enact themselves; I see at the dead of night pale heads crane from the window, oppressive silence hold the room, as some dim and ugly burden jerks and dangles from the descending rope, while the rude gear creaks and rustles, and the vane upon the cupola sings its melancholy rusty song in the glimmering darkness. It is strange that the mind should be so tangibly impressed and yet should have no power given it to solve the sad enigma.

24
Sep. 10, 1891.

The Country
Very few consecutive days pass at Golden End without my contriving to get what I most enjoy in the form of exercise—a long, slow, solitary ride; severer activities are denied me. I have a strong, big-boned, amiable horse—strength is the one desideratum in a horse, in country where, to reach a point that appears to be a quarter of a mile away, it is often necessary to descend by a steep lane to a point two or three hundred feet below and to ascend a corresponding acclivity on the other side. Sometimes my ride has a definite object. I have to see a neighbouring farmer on business, or there is shopping to be done at Spyfield, or a distant call has to be paid—but it is best when there is no such scheme—and the result is that after a few years there is hardly a lane within a radius of five miles that I have not carefully explored and hardly a hamlet within ten miles that I have not visited.

The by-lanes are the most attractive feature. You turn out of the high-road down a steep sandy track, with high banks overhung by hazel and spindlewood and oak-copse; the ground falls rapidly. Through gaps at the side you can see the high, sloping forest glades opposite, or look along lonely green rides which lead straight into the heart of silent woods. There has been as a rule no parsimonious policy of enclosure, and the result is that there are often wide grassy spaces beside the road, thick-set with furze or forest undergrowth, with here and there a tiny pool, or a little dingle where sandstone has been dug. Down at the base of the hill you find a stream running deep below a rustic white-railed bridge, through sandy cuttings, all richly embowered with alders, and murmuring pleasantly through tall water-plants. Here and there is a weather-tiled cottage, with a boarded gable and a huge brick chimney-stack, flanked by a monstrous yew. Suddenly the road strikes into a piece of common, a true English forest, with a few huge beeches, and thick covert of ferns and saplings; still higher and you are on open ground, with the fragrant air blowing off the heather; a clump of pines marks the summit, and in an instant the rolling plain lies before you, rich in wood, rising in billowy ranges, with the smoke going up from a hundred hamlets, and the shadowy downs closing the horizon. Then you can ride a mile or two on soft white sand-paths winding in and out among the heather, while the sun goes slowly down among purple islands of cloud, with gilded promontories and fiords of rosy light, and the landscape grows more and more indistinct and romantic, suffused in a golden haze. At last it is time to turn homewards, and you wind down into a leafy dingle, where the air lies in cool strata across the sun-warmed path, and fragrant wood-smells, from the heart of winding ways and marshy streamlets, pour out of the green dusk. The whole day you have hardly seen a human being—an old labourer has looked out with a slow bovine stare from some field-corner, a group of cottage children have hailed you over a fence, or a carter walking beside a clinking team has given you a muttered greeting—the only sounds have been the voices of birds breaking from the thicket, the rustle of leaves, the murmuring of unseen streams, and the padding of your horse's hoofs in the sandy lane.

The Peaceful Mind

And what does the mind do in these tranquil hours? I hardly know. The thought runs in a little leisurely stream, glancing from point to point; the observation is, I notice, prematurely acute, and, though the intellectual faculties are in abeyance, drinks in impressions with greedy delight: the feathery, blue-green foliage of the ash-suckers, the grotesque, geometrical forms in the lonely sandstone quarry, the curving water-meadows with their tousled grasses, the stone-leek on the roof of mellowed barns, the flash of white chalk-quarries carved out of distant downs, the climbing, clustering roofs of the hamlet on the neighbouring ridge.

Some would say that the mind in such hours grows dull, narrow, rustical, and slow—"in the lonely vale of streams," as Ossian sang, "abides the narrow soul." I hardly know, but I think it is the opposite: it is true that one does not learn in such silent hours the deft trick of speech, the easy flow of humorous thoughts, the tinkling interchange of the mind; but there creeps over the spirit something of the coolness of the pasture, the tranquillity of green copses, and the contentment of the lazy stream. I think that, undiluted, such days might foster the elementary brutishness of the spirit, and that just as rhododendrons degenerate, if untended, to the primal magenta type, so one might revert by slow degrees to the animal which lies not far below the civilised surface. But there is no danger in my own life that I should have too much of such reverie; indeed, I have to scheme a little for it; and it is to me a bath of peace, a plunge into the quiet waters of nature, a refreshing return to the untroubled and gentle spirit of the earth.

The only thing to fear in such rides as these, is if some ugly or sordid thought, some muddy difficulty, some tangled dilemma is stuck like a burr on the mind; then indeed such hours are of little use, if they be not positively harmful. The mind (at least my mind) has a way of arranging matters in solitude so as to be as little hopeful, as little kindly as possible; the fretted spirit brews its venom, practises for odious repartees, plans devilish questions, and rehearses the mean drama over and over. At such hours I feel indeed like Sinbad, with the lithe legs and skinny arms of the Old Man of the Sea twined round his neck. But the mood changes—an interesting letter, a sunshiny day, a pleasant visitor—any of these raises the spirit out of the mire, and restores me to myself; and I resume my accustomed tranquillity all the more sedulously for having had a dip in the tonic tide of depression.

25
June 6, 1892.

I have often thought what a lightening of the load of life it would be if we could arrive at greater simplicity and directness in our social dealings with others. Of course the first difficulty to triumph over is the physical difficulty of simple shyness, which so often paralyses men and women in the presence of a stranger. But how instantly and perfectly a natural person evokes naturalness in others. This naturalness is hardly to be achieved without a certain healthy egotism. It by no means produces naturalness in others to begin operations by questioning people about themselves. But if one person begins to talk easily and frankly about his own interests, others insensibly follow suit by a kind of simple imitativeness. And if the inspirer of this naturalness is not a profound egotist, if he is really interested in other people, if he can waive his own claims to attention, the difficulty is overcome.

The Conveyancer
The other day I was bicycling, and on turning out of Spyfield, where I had been doing some business, I observed another bicyclist a little ahead of me. He was a tall thin man, with a loose white hat, and he rode with a certain fantastic childish zest which attracted my attention. If there was a little upward slope in the road, he tacked extravagantly from side to side, and

seemed to be encouraging himself by murmured exhortations. He had a word for every one he passed. I rode for about half a mile behind him, and he at last dismounted at the foot of a steep slope that leads up to a place called Gallows Hill. He stopped half-way up the hill to study a map, and as I passed him wheeling my bicycle, he called cheerily to me to ask how far it was to a neighbouring village. I told him to the best of my ability, whereupon he said, "Oh no, I am sure you are wrong; it must be twice that distance!" I was for an instant somewhat nettled, feeling that if he knew the distance, his question had a certain wantonness. So I said, "Well, I have lived here for twenty years and know all the roads very well." The stranger touched his hat and said, "I am sure I apologise with all my heart; I ought not to have spoken as I did."

Examining him at my leisure I saw him to be a tall, lean man, with rather exaggerated features. He had a big, thin head, a long, pointed nose, a mobile and smiling mouth, large dark eyes, and full side-whiskers. I took him at once for a professional man of some kind, solicitor, schoolmaster, or even a clergyman, though his attire was not clerical. "Here," he said, "just take the end of this map and let us consult together." I did as I was desired, and he pointed out the way he meant to take. "Now," he said, "there is a train there in an hour, and I want to arrive there easily—mind you, not hot; that is so uncomfortable." I told him that if he knew the road, which was a complicated one, he could probably just do it in the time; but I added that I was myself going to pass a station on the line, where he might catch the same train nearer town. He looked at me with a certain slyness. "Are you certain of that?" he cried; "I have all the trains at my fingers' ends." I assured him it was so, while he consulted a time-table. "Right!" he said, "you are right, but all the trains do not stop there; it is not a deduction that you can draw from the fact of one stopping at the other station." We walked up to the top of the hill together, and I proposed that we should ride in company. He accepted with alacrity. "Nothing I should like better!" As we got on to our bicycles his foot slipped. "You will notice," he said, "that these are new boots—of a good pattern—but somewhat smooth on the sole; in fact they slip." I replied that it was a good thing to scratch new boots on the sole, so as to roughen them before riding. "A capital idea!" he said delightedly; "I shall do it the moment I return, with a pair of nail-scissors, closed, mind you, to prevent my straining either blade." We then rode off, and after a few yards he said, "Now, this is not my usual pace—rather faster than I can go with comfort." I begged him to take his own pace, and he then began to talk of the country. "Pent up in my chambers," he said—"I am a conveyancer, you must know—I long for a green lane and a row of elms. I have lived for years in town, in a most convenient street, I must tell you, but I sicken for the country; and now that I am in easier circumstances—I have lived a hard life, mind you—I am going to make the great change, and live in the country. Now, what is your opinion of the relative merits of town and country as a place of residence?" I told him that the only disadvantage of the country to my mind was the difficulty of servants. "Right again!" he said, as if I had answered a riddle. "But I have overcome that; I have been educating a pair of good maids for years—they are paragons, and they will go anywhere with me; indeed, they prefer the country themselves."

In such light talk we beguiled the way; too soon we came to where our roads divided; I pointed out to him the turn he was to take. "Well," he said cheerily, "all pleasant things come to an end. I confess that I have enjoyed your company, and am grateful for your kind communications; perhaps we may have another encounter, and if not, we will be glad to have met, and think sometimes of this pleasant hour!" He put his foot upon the step of his bicycle cautiously, then mounted gleefully, and saying "Good-bye, good-bye!" he waved his hand, and in a moment was out of sight.

The thought of this brave and merry spirit planning schemes of life, making the most of simple pleasures, has always dwelt with me. The gods, as we know from Homer, assumed the forms of men, and were at the pains to relate long and wholly unreliable stories to account for their presence at particular times and places; and I have sometimes wondered whether in the lean conveyancer, with his childlike zest for experience, his brisk enjoyment of the smallest details of daily life, I did not entertain some genial, masquerading angel unawares.

26
June 8, 1893.

Is it not the experience of every one that at rare intervals, by some happy accident, life presents one with a sudden and delicious thrill of beauty? I have often tried to analyse the constituent elements of these moments, but the essence is subtle and defies detection. They cannot be calculated upon, or produced by any amount of volition or previous preparation. One thing about these tiny ecstasies I have noticed—they do not come as a rule when one is tranquil, healthy, serene—they rather come as a compensation for weariness and discontent; and yet they are the purest gold of life, and a good deal of sand is well worth washing for a pellet or two of the real metal.

To-day I was more than usually impatient; over me all the week had hung the shadow of some trying, difficult business—the sort of business which, whatever you do, will be done to nobody's satisfaction. After a vain attempt to wrestle with it, I gave it up, and went out on a bicycle; the wind blew gently and steadily this soft June day; all the blue sky was filled with large white clouds, blackening to rain. I made for the one piece of flat ground in our neighbourhood. It is tranquillising, I have often found, to the dweller in a hilly land, to cool and sober the eye occasionally with the pure breadths of a level plain. The grass was thick and heavy-headed in the fields, but of mere wantonness I turned down a lane which I know has no ending,—a mere relief-road for carts to have access to a farm,—and soon came to the end of it in a small grassy circle, with a cottage or two, where a footpath strikes off across the fields.

Heretofore Unvisited

Why did I never come here before, I thought. Through a gap in the hedge I saw a large broad pasture, fringed in the far distance with full-foliaged, rotund elms in thick leaf; a row of willows on the horizon marked the track of a stream. In the pasture in front of me was a broad oblong pool of water with water-lilies; down one side ran a row of huge horse-chestnuts, and the end was rich in elders full of flat white cakes of blossom. In the field grazed an old horse; while a pigeon sailed lazily down from the trees and ran to the pool to drink. That was all there was to see. But it brought me with a deep and inexplicable thrill close to the heart of the old, kindly, patient Earth, the mother and the mistress and the servant of all—she who allows us to tear and rend her for our own paltry ends, and then sets, how sweetly and tranquilly, to work, with what a sense of inexhaustible leisure, to paint and mellow and adorn the rude and bleeding gaps. We tear up a copse, and she fills the ugly scars in the spring with a crop of fresh flowers—of flowers, perhaps, which are not seen in the neighbourhood, but whose seeds have lain vital and moist in the ground, but too deep to know the impulse born of the spring sun. Yet now they burst their armoured mail, and send a thin, white, worm-like arm to the top, which, as soon as it passes into the light, drinks from the rays the green flush that it chooses to hide its nakedness. We dig a pool in the crumbling marl. At the time the wound seems irreparable; the ugly, slobbered banks grin at us like death; the ground is full of footprints and slime, broken roots and bedabbled leaves,—and next year it is all a paradise of green and luscious water-plants, with a hundred quiet lives being lived there, of snail and worm and beetle, as though the place had never been disturbed. We build a raw red house with an insupportably geometrical outline, the hue of the vicious fire still in the bricks; pass fifty years, and the bricks are mellow and soft, plastered with orange rosettes or grey filaments of lichen; the ugly window frames are blistered and warped; the roof has taken a soft and yielding outline—all is in peace and harmony with the green world in which it sits.

The Repairer of the Breach

I never saw this more beautifully illustrated than once, when a great house in Whitehall was destroyed, and heaped up in a hideous rockery of bricks. All through the winter these raw ruins, partly concealed by a rough hoarding, tainted the view; but as soon as spring returned, from every inch of grit rose a forest of green stalks of willow-herb, each in summer to be crowned with a spire of fantastic crimson flowers, and to pass a little later into those graceful, ghostly husks that shiver in the wind. Centuries must have passed since willow-herb had grown on that spot. Had they laid dormant, these hopeful seeds, or had they been wafted along dusty streets and high in air over sun-scorched spaces? Nature at all events had seen her chance, and done her work patiently and wisely as ever.

But to return to my lane-end. How strange and deep are the impressions of a deep and inviolate peace that some quiet corner like this gives to the restless spirit! It can never be so with the scenes that have grown familiar, where we have carried about with us the burden of private cares—the symptoms of the disease of life. In any house where we have lived, every corner, however peaceful and beautiful in itself, is bound to be gradually soaked, as it were, in the miseries of life, to conceal its beauties under the accretion of sordid associations.

This room we connect with some sad misunderstanding. There we gave way to some petty passion of resentment, of jealousy, of irritation, or vainly tried to pacify some similar outbreak from one we loved. This is the torture of imagination; to feel the beauty of sight and sound, we must be sensitive; and if we are sensitive, we carry about the shadow with us—the capacity for self-torment, the struggle of the ideal with the passing mood.

Sad Associations

I have sometimes climbed to the top of a hill and looked into some unknown and placid valley, with field and wood and rivulet and the homes of men. I have seen the figures of men and oxen move sedately about those quiet fields. Often, too, gliding at evening in a train through a pastoral country when the setting sun bathes all things in genial light and contented shade, I have felt the same thought. "How peaceful, how simple life would be, nay, must be, here." Only very gradually, as life goes on, does it dawn upon the soul that the trouble lies deeper, and that though surrounded by the most unimagined peace, the same fret, the same beating of restless wings, the same delays attend. That dreamt-of peace can hardly be attained. The most we can do is to enjoy it to the utmost when it is with us; and when it takes its flight, and leaves us dumb, discontented, peevish, to quench the sordid thought in resolute silence, to curb the grating mood, to battle mutely with the cowering fear; and so to escape investing the house and the garden that we love with the poisonous and bitter associations that strike the beauty out of the fairest scene.

27
September 20, 1894.

I had to-day a strange little instance of the patient, immutable habit of nature. Some years ago there was a particular walk of which I was fond; it led through pastures, by shady wood-ends, and came out eventually on a bridge that spanned the line. Here I often went to see a certain express pass; there was something thrilling in the silent cutting, the beckoning, ghostly arm of the high signal, the faint far-off murmur, and then the roar of the great train forging past. It was a breath from the world.

The Red Spider
On the parapet of the bridge, grey with close-grained lichen, there lived a numerous colony of little crimson spiders. What they did I never could discern; they wandered aimlessly about hither and thither, in a sort of feeble, blind haste; if they ever encountered each other on their rambles, they stopped, twiddled horns, and fled in a sudden horror; they never seemed to eat or sleep, and even continued their endless peregrinations in the middle of heavy showers, which flicked them quivering to death.

I used to amuse myself with thinking how one had but to alter the scale, so to speak, and what appalling, intolerable monsters these would become. Think of it! huge crimson shapeless masses, with strong wiry legs, and waving mandibles, tramping silently over the grey veldt, and perhaps preying on minute luckless insects, which would flee before them in vain.

One day I walked on ahead, leaving a companion to follow. He did follow, and joined me on the bridge—bringing heavy tidings which had just arrived after I left home.

The place grew to me so inseparably connected with the horror of the news that I instinctively abandoned it; but to-day, finding myself close to the place—nearly ten years had passed without my visiting it—I turned aside, musing on the old sadness, with something in my heart of the soft regret that a sorrow wears when seen through the haze of years.

There was the place, just the same; I bent to see a passing train and (I had forgotten all about them) there were my red spiders still pursuing their aimless perambulations. But who can tell the dynasties, the genealogies that had bridged the interval?

The red spider has no great use in the world, as far as I know. But he has every right to be there, and to enjoy the sun falling so warm on the stone. I wonder what he thinks about it all? For me, he has become the type of the patient, pretty fancies of nature, so persistently pursued, so void of moral, so deliciously fantastic and useless—but after all, what am I to talk of usefulness?

Spider and man, man and spider—and to the pitying, tender mind of God, the brisk spider on his ledge, and the dull, wistful, middle-aged man who loiters looking about him, wondering and waiting, are much the same. He has a careful thought of each, I know:—

To both alike the darkness and the day,
The sunshine and the flowers,
We draw sad comfort, thinking we obey
A deeper will than ours.

28
August 4, 1895.

The Dawn
Just another picture lingers with me, for no very defined reason. It was an August night; I had gone to rest with the wind sighing and buffeting against my windows, but when I awoke with a start, deep in the night, roused, it seemed, as by footsteps in the air and a sudden hollow calling of airy voices, it was utterly still outside. I drew aside my heavy tapestry curtain, and lo! it was the dawn. A faint upward gush of lemon-coloured light edged the eastern hills. The air as I threw the casement wide was unutterably sweet and cool. In the faint light, over the roof of the great barn, I saw what I had seen a hundred times before, a quiet wood-end, upon which the climbing hedges converge. But now it seemed to lie there in a pure and silent dream, sleeping a light sleep, waiting contentedly for the dawn and smiling softly to itself. Over the fields lay little wreaths of mist, and beyond the wood, hills of faintest blue, the hills of dreamland, where it seems as if no harsh wind

could blow or cold rain fall. I felt as though I stood to watch the stainless slumber of one I loved, and was permitted by some happy and holy chance to see for once the unuttered peace that earth enjoys in her lonely and unwatched hours. Too often, alas! one carries into the fairest scenes a turmoil of spirit, a clouded mind that breaks and mars the spell. But here it was not so; I gazed upon the hushed eyes of the earth, and heard her sleeping breath; and, as the height of blessing, I seemed myself to have left for a moment the past behind, to have no overshadowing from the future, but to live only in the inviolate moment, clear-eyed and clean-hearted, to see the earth in her holiest and most secluded sanctuary, unsuspicious and untroubled, bathed in the light and careless slumber of eternal youth, in that delicious oblivion that fences day from weary day.

In the jaded morning light the glory was faded, and the little wood wore its usual workaday look, the face it bears before the world; but I, I had seen it in its golden dreams; I knew its secret, and it could not deceive me; it had yielded to me unawares its sublimest confidence, and however it might masquerade as a commonplace wood, a covert for game, a commercial item in an estate-book, known by some homely name, I had seen it once undisguised, and knew it as one of the porches of heaven.

29
April 4, 1896.

It seems a futile task to say anything about the spring; yet poets and romancers make no apologies for treating of love, which is an old and familiar phenomenon enough. And I declare that the wonder of spring, so far from growing familiar, strikes upon the mind with a bewildering strangeness, a rapturous surprise, which is greater every year. Every spring I say to myself that I never realised before what a miraculous, what an astounding thing is the sudden conspiracy of trees and flowers, hatched so insensibly, and carried out so punctually, to leap into life and loveliness together. The velvety softness of the grass, the mist of green that hangs about the copse, the swift weaving of the climbing tapestry that screens the hedgerow-banks, the jewellery of flowers that sparkle out of all sequestered places; they are adorable. But this early day of spring is close and heavy, with a slow rain dropping reluctantly out of the sky, a day when an insidious melancholy lies in wait for human beings, a sense of inadequacy, a meek rebellion against all activity, bodily or mental. I walk slowly and sedately along the sandy roads fast oozing into mire. There is a sense of expectancy in the air; tree and flower are dispirited too, oppressed with heaviness, and yet gratefully conscious, as I am not, of the divine storage of that pure and subtle element that is taking place for their benefit. "Praise God," said Saint Francis, "for our sister the water, for she is very serviceable to us and humble and clean." Yes, we give thanks! but, alas! to sit still and be pumped into, as Carlyle said of Coleridge's conversation, can never be an enlivening process.

Yet would that the soul could gratefully recognise her own rainy days; could droop, like Nature, with patient acquiescence, with wise passivity, till the wells of strength and freshness are stored!

Subtle Superiorities
The particular form of melancholy which I find besets me on these sad reflective mornings, is to compare my vague ambitions with my concrete performances. I will not say that in my dreamful youth I cherished the idea of swaying the world. I never expected to play a brave part on the public stage. Political and military life—the two careers which ripple communities to the verge, never came within the range of my possibilities. But I think that I was conscious—as most intelligent young creatures undoubtedly are—of a subtle superiority to other people. An ingenious preacher once said that we cannot easily delude ourselves into the belief that we are richer, taller, more handsome, or even wiser, better, abler, and more capable than other people, but we can and do very easily nourish a secret belief that we are more interesting than others. Such an illusion has a marvellous vitality; it has a delicate power of resisting the rude lessons to the contrary which contact with the world would teach us; and I should hardly like to confess how ill I have learned my lesson. I realise, of course, that I have done little to establish this superiority in the eyes of others; but I find it hard to disabuse myself of the vague belief that if only I had the art of more popular and definite expression, if only the world had a little more leisure to look in sequestered nooks for delicate flowers of thought and temperament, then it might be realized how exquisite a nature is here neglected.

The Hard Truth
In saying this I am admitting the reader to the inmost penetralia of thought. I frankly confess that in my robust and equable moments I do recognise the broken edge of my life, and what a very poor thing I have made of it—but, for all that, it is my honest belief that we most of us have in our hearts that inmost shrine of egotism, where the fire burns clear and fragrant before an idealised image of self; and I go further, and say that I believe this to be a wholesome and valuable thing, because it is of the essence of self-respect, and gives us a feeble impulse in the direction of virtue and faith. If a man ever came to realise exactly his place in the world,

as others realise it, how feeble, how uninteresting, how ludicrously unnecessary he is, and with what a speedy unconcern others would accommodate themselves to his immediate disappearance, he would sink into an abyss of gloom out of which nothing would lift him. It is one of the divine uses of love, that it glorifies life by restoring and raising one's self-esteem.

In the dejected reveries of such languorous spring days as these, no such robust egotism as I have above represented comes to my aid. I see myself stealing along, a shy, tarnished thing, a blot among the fresh hopes and tender dreams that smile on every bank. The pitiful fabric of my life is mercilessly unveiled; here I loiter, a lonely, shabby man, bruised by contact with the word, dilatory, dumb, timid, registering tea-table triumphs, local complacencies, provincial superiorities—spending sheltered days in such comfortable dreams as are born of warm fires, ample meals, soft easy-chairs, and congratulating myself on poetical potentialities, without any awkward necessities of translating my dreams into corrective action—or else discharging homely duties with an almost sacerdotal solemnity, and dignifying with the title of religious quietism what is done by hundreds of people instinctively and simply and without pretentiousness. If I raved against my limitations, deemed my cage a prison, beat myself sick against the bars, I might then claim to be a fiery and ardent soul; but I cannot honestly do this; and I must comfort myself with the thought that possibly the ill-health, which necessitates my retirement, compensates for the disabilities it inflicts on me, by removing the stimulus which would make my prison insupportable.

In this agreeable frame of mind I drew near home and stood awhile on the deserted bowling-green with its elder-thickets, its little grassy terraces, its air of regretful wildness, so often worn by a place that has been tamed by civilisation and has not quite reverted to its native savagery. A thrush sang with incredible clearness, repeating a luscious phrase often enough to establish its precision of form, and yet not often enough to satiate—a triumph of instinctive art.

These thrushes are great favourites of mine; I often sit, on a dewy morning, to watch them hunting. They hop lightly along, till they espy a worm lying in blissful luxury out of his hole; two long hops, and they are upon him; he, using all his retractile might, clings to his home, but the thrush sets his feet firm in the broad stride of the Greek warrior, gives a mighty tug—you can see the viscous elastic thread strain—and the worm is stretched writhing on the grass. What are the dim dreams of the poor reptile, I wonder; does he regret his cool burrow, "and youth and strength and this delightful world?"—no, I think it is a stoical resignation. For a moment the thrush takes no notice of him, but surveys the horizon with a caution which the excitement of the chase has for an instant imprudently diverted. Then the meal begins, with horrid leisureliness.

But it is strange to note the perpetual instinctive consciousness of danger which besets birds thus in the open; they must live in a tension of nervous watchfulness which would depress a human being into melancholia. There is no absorbed gobbling; between every mouthful the little head with its beady eyes swings right and left to see that all is clear; and he is for ever changing his position and seldom fronts the same way for two seconds together.

Do we realise what it must be to live, as even these sheltered birds do in a quiet garden, with the fear of attack and death hanging over them from morning to night?

The Bondage of a Bird
Another fact that these thrushes have taught me is the extreme narrowness of their self-chosen world. They are born and live within the compass of a few yards. We are apt to envy a bird the power of changing his horizon, of soaring above the world, and choosing for his home the one spot he desires. Think what our life would be if, without luggage, without encumbrances, we could rise in the air and, winging our way out to the horizon, choose some sequestered valley, and there, without house, without rates and taxes, abide, with water babbling in its channel and food abundant. Yet it is far otherwise. One of my thrushes has a white feather in his wing; he was hatched out in a big syringa which stands above the bowling-green; and though I have observed the birds all about my few acres carefully enough I have never seen this particular thrush anywhere but on the lawn. He never seems even to cross the wall into the garden; he has a favourite bush to roost in, and another where he sometimes sings: at times he beats along the privet hedge, or in the broad border, but he generally hops about the lawn, and I do not think he has ever ventured beyond it. He works hard for his living too; he is up at dawn, and till early afternoon he is generally engaged in foraging. He will die, I suppose, in the garden, though how his body is disposed of is a mystery to me.

The Soul of a Thrush
He takes the limitations of his life just as he finds them; he never seems to think he would like to be otherwise; but he works diligently for his living, he sings a grateful song, he sleeps well, he does not compare himself with other birds or wish his lot was different—he has no regrets, no hopes, and

few cares. Still less has he any philanthropic designs of raising the tone of his brother thrushes, or directing a mission among the quarrelsome sparrows. Sometimes he fights a round or two, and when the spring comes, stirred by delicious longings, he will build a nest, devote the food he would like to devour to his beady-eyed, yellow-lipped young, and die as he has lived. There is a good deal to be said for this brave and honest life, and especially for the bright and wholesome music which he makes within the thickets. I do not know that it can be improved upon.

30
Aug. 19, 1898.

God's Acre
There is a simple form of expedition of which I am very fond; that is the leisurely visiting of some rustic church in the neighbourhood. They are often very beautifully placed—sometimes they stand high on the ridges and bear a bold testimony to the faith; sometimes they lie nestled in trees, hidden in valleys, as if to show it is possible to be holy and beautiful, though unseen. Sometimes they are the central ornament of a village street; there generally seems some simple and tender reason for their position; but the more populous their neighbourhood, the more they have suffered from the zeal of the restorer. What I love best of all is a church that stands a little apart, sheltered in wood, dreaming by itself, and guarding its tranquil and grateful secret—"secretum meum mihi," it seems to say.

I like to loiter in the churchyard ground to step over the hillocks, to read the artless epitaphs on slanting tombs; it is not a morbid taste, for if there is one feeling more than another that such a visit removes and tranquillises, it is the fear of death. Death here appears in its most peaceful light; it seems so necessary, so common, so quiet and inevitable an end, like a haven after a troubled sea. Here all the sad and unhappy incidents of mortality are forgotten, and death appears only in the light of a tender and dreamful sleep.

Better still is the grateful coolness of the church itself; here one can trace in the epitaphs the fortunes of a family—one can see the graves of old squires who have walked over their own fields, talked with their neighbours, shot, hunted, eaten, drunk, have loved and been loved, and have yielded their place in the fulness of days to those that have come after them. Very moving, too, are the evidences of the sincere grief, which underlies the pompous phraseology of the marble monument with its urns and cherubs. I love to read the long list of homely virtues attributed by the living to the dead in the depth of sorrow, and to believe them true. Then there are records of untimely deaths,—the young wife, the soldier in his prime, the boy or girl who have died unstained by life, and about whom clings the passionate remembrance of the happy days that are no more. Such records as those do not preach the lesson of vanity and decay, but the lesson of pure and grateful resignation, the faith that the God who made the world so beautiful, and filled it so full of happiness, has surprises in store for His children, in a world undreamed of.

The Monument
One monument in a church not far from Golden End always brings tears to my eyes; there is a chapel in the aisle, the mausoleum of an ancient family, where mouldering banners and pennons hang in the gloom; in the centre of the chapel is an altar-tomb, on which lies the figure of a young boy, thirteen years old, the inscription says. He reclines on one arm, he has a delicately carved linen shirt that leaves the slender neck free, and he is wrapped in a loose gown; he looks upward toward the east, his long hair falling over his shoulders, his thin and shapely hand upon his knee. On each side of the tomb, kneeling on marble cushions on the ledge, are his father and mother, an earl and countess. The mother, in the stately costume of a bygone court, with hair carefully draped, watches the face of the child with a look in which love seems to have cast out grief. The earl in armour, a strongly-built, soldier-like figure, looks across the boy's knee at his wife's face, but in his expression—I know not if it be art—there seems to be a look of rebellious sorrow, of thwarted pride. All his wealth and state could not keep his darling with him, and he does not seem to understand. There have they knelt, the little group, for over two centuries, waiting and watching, and one is glad to think that they know now whatever there is to know. Outside the golden afternoon slants across the headstones, and the birds twitter in the ivy, while a full stream winds below through the meadows that once were theirs.

Such a contemplation does not withdraw one from life or tend to give a false view of its energies; it does not forbid one to act, to love, to live; it only gilds with a solemn radiance the cloud that overshadows us all, the darkness of the inevitable end. Face to face with the lacrimæ rerum in so simple and tender a form, the heavy words Memento Mori fall upon the heart not as a sad and harsh interruption of wordly dreams and fancies, but as a deep pedal note upon a sweet organ, giving strength and fulness and balance to the dying away of the last grave and gentle chord.

31
If any one whose eye may fall upon these pages be absolutely equable of temperament, serene, contented, the same one day as another, as Dr. Johnson said of Reynolds, let him not read this chapter—he will think it a mere cry in the dark, better smothered in the bed-clothes, an unmanly piece of morbid pathology, a secret and sordid disease better undivulged, on which all persons of proper pride should hold their peace.

Well, it is not for him that I write; there are books and books, and even chapters and chapters, just as there are people and people. I myself avoid books dealing with health and disease. I used when younger to be unable to resist the temptation of a medical book; but now I am wiser, and if I sometimes yield to the temptation, it is with a backward glancing eye and a cautious step. And I will say that I generally put back the book with a snap, in a moment, as though a snake had stung me. But there will be no pathology here—nothing but a patient effort to look a failing in the face, and to suggest a remedy.

Fears
I speak to the initiated, to those who have gone down into the dark cave, and seen the fire burn low in the shrine, and watched aghast the formless, mouldering things—hideous implements are they, or mere weapons?—that hang upon the walls.

Do you know what it is to dwell, perhaps for days together, under the shadow of a fear? Perhaps a definite fear—a fear of poverty, or a fear of obloquy, or a fear of harshness, or a fear of pain, or a fear of disease—or, worse than all, a boding, misshapen, sullen dread which has no definite cause, and is therefore the harder to resist.

Dreams
These moods, I say it with gratitude for myself and for the encouragement of others, tend to diminish in acuteness and in frequency as I grow older. They are now, as ever, preluded by dreams of a singular kind, dreams of rapid and confused action, dreams of a romantic and exaggerated pictorial character—huge mountain ranges, lofty and venerable buildings, landscapes of incredible beauty, gardens of unimaginable luxuriance, which pass with incredible rapidity before the mind. I will indicate two of these in detail. I was in a vessel like a yacht, armed with a massive steel prow like a ram, which moved in some aerial fashion over a landscape, skimming it seemed to me but a few feet above the ground. A tall man of benignant aspect stood upon the bridge, and directed the operations of the unseen

navigator. We ascended a heathery valley, and presently encountered snow-drifts, upon which the vessel seemed to settle down to her full speed; at last we entered a prodigious snowfield, with vast ridged snow-waves extending in every direction for miles; the vessel ran not over but through these waves, sending up huge spouts of snow which fell in cool showers upon my head and hands, while the tinkle of dry ice fragments made a perpetual low music. At last we stopped and I descended on to the plateau. Far ahead, through rolling clouds, I saw the black snow-crowned heights of a mountain, loftier than any seen by human eye, and for leagues round me lay the interminable waste of snow. I was aroused from my absorption by a voice behind me; the vessel started again on her course with a leap like a porpoise, and though I screamed aloud to stop her, I saw her, in a few seconds, many yards ahead, describing great curves as she ran, with the snow spouting over her like a fountain.

The second was a very different scene. I was in the vine-clad alleys of some Italian garden; against the still blue air a single stone pine defined itself; I walked along a path, and turning a corner an exquisite conventual building of immense size, built of a light brown stone, revealed itself. From all the alleys round emerged troops of monastic figures in soft white gowns, and a mellow chime of exceeding sweetness floated from the building. I saw that I too was robed like the rest; but the gliding figures outstripped me; and arriving last at a great iron portal I found it closed, and the strains of a great organ came drowsily from within.

Then into the dream falls a sudden sense of despair like an ashen cloud; a feeling of incredible agony, intensified by the beauty of the surrounding scene, that agony which feverishly questions as to why so dark a stroke should fall when the mind seems at peace with itself and lost in dreamy wonder at the loveliness all about it. Then the vision closes, and for a time the mind battles with dark waves of anguish, emerging at last, like a diver from a dim sea, into the waking consciousness. The sickly daylight filters through the window curtains and the familiar room swims into sight. The first thought is one of unutterable relief, which is struck instantly out of the mind by the pounce of the troubled mood; and then follows a ghastly hour, when every possibility of horror and woe intangible presses in upon the battling mind. At such moments a definite difficulty, a practical problem would be welcome—but there is none; the misery is too deep for thought, and even, when after long wrestling, the knowledge comes that it is all a subjective condition, and that there is no adequate cause in life or circumstances for this unmanning terror—even then it can only be silently endured, like the racking of some fierce physical pain.

Woe

The day that succeeds to such a waking mood is almost the worst part of the experience. Shaken and dizzied by the inrush of woe, the mind struggles wearily through hour after hour; the familiar duties are intolerable; food has no savour; action and thought no interest; and if for an hour the tired head is diverted by some passing event, or if, oppressed with utter exhaustion, it sinks into an unrefreshing slumber, repose but gives the strength to suffer—the accursed mood leaps again, as from an unseen lair, upon the unnerved consciousness, and tears like some strange beast the helpless and palpitating soul.

When first, at Cambridge, I had the woeful experiences above recorded, I was so unused to endurance, so bewildered by suffering, that I think for awhile I was almost beside myself. I recollect going down with some friends, in a brief lull of misery, to watch a football match, when the horror seized me in the middle of a cheerful talk with such vehemence, that I could only rush off with a muttered word, and return to my rooms, in which I immured myself to spend an hour in an agony of prayer. Again I recollect sitting with some of the friends of my own age after hall; we were smoking and talking peacefully enough—for some days my torment had been suspended—when all at once, out of the secret darkness the terror leapt upon me, and after in vain resisting it for a few moments, I hurried away, having just enough self-respect to glance at my watch and mutter something about a forgotten engagement. But worst of all was a walk taken with my closest friend on a murky November day. We started in good spirits, when in a moment the accursed foe was upon me; I hardly spoke except for fitful questions. Our way led us to a level crossing, beside a belt of woodland, where a huge luggage train was jolting and bumping backwards and forewards. We hung upon the gate; and then, and then only, came upon me in a flash an almost irresistible temptation to lay my head beneath the ponderous wheels, and end it all; I could only pray in silence, and hurry from the spot in speechless agitation. What wonder if I heard on the following day that my friend complained that I was altering for the worse—that I had become so sullen and morose that it was no use talking to me.

Gradually, very gradually, the aching frost of the soul broke up and thawed; little trifling encouraging incidents—a small success or two, an article accepted by a magazine, a friendship, an athletic victory, raised me step by step out of the gloom. One benefit, even at the time, it brought me—an acute sensitiveness to beauty both of sight and sound. I used to steal at even-song into the dark nave of King's Chapel, and the sight of the screen, the flood of subdued light overflowing from the choir, the carven angels with their gilded trumpets, penetrated into the soul with an exquisite sweetness; and still more the music—whether the low prelude with the whispering pedals, the severe monotone breaking into freshets of harmony, the swing and richness of the chants, or the elaborate beauty of some familiar magnificat or anthem—all fell like showers upon the arid sense. The music at King's had one characteristic that I have never heard elsewhere; the properties of the building are such that the echo lingers without blurring the successive chords—not "loth to die," I used to think, as Wordsworth says, but sinking as it were from consciousness to dream, and from dream to death.

The Brotherhood of Sorrow
One further gain—the greater—was that my suffering did not, I think, withdraw me wholly into myself and fence me from the world; rather it gave me a sense of the brotherhood of grief. I was one with all the agonies that lie silent in the shadow of life; and though my suffering had no tangible cause, yet I was initiated into the fellowship of those who bear. I understood;— weak, faithless, and faulty as I was, I was no longer in the complacent isolation of the strong, the successful, the selfish, and even in my darkest hour I had strength to thank God for that.

32
Oct. 21, 1898.

I have been reading some of my old diaries to-day; and I am tempted to try and disentangle, as far as I can, the motif that seems to me to underlie my simple life.

One question above all others has constantly recurred to my mind; and the answer to it is the sum of my slender philosophy.

The question then is this: is a simple, useful, dignified, happy life possible to most of us without the stimulus of affairs, of power, of fame? I answer unhesitatingly that such a life is possible. The tendency of the age is to measure success by publicity, not to think highly of any person or any work unless it receives "recognition," to think it essential to happiness monstrari digito, to be in the swim, to be a personage.

I admit at once the temptation; to such successful persons comes the consciousness of influence, the feeling of power, the anxious civilities of the undistinguished, the radiance of self-respect, the atmosphere of flattering, subtle deference, the seduction of which not even the most independent and noble characters can escape. Indeed, many an influential man of simple character and unpretending virtue, who rates such conveniences of life at their true value, and does not pursue them as an end, would be disagreeably conscious of the lack of these petits soins if he adopted an unpopular cause or for any reason forfeited the influence which begets them.

A friend of mine came to see me the other day fresh from a visit to a great house. His host was a man of high cabinet rank, the inheritor of an ample fortune and a historic name, who has been held by his nearest friends to cling to political life longer than prudence would warrant. My friend told me that he had been left alone one evening with his host, who had, half humorously, half seriously, indulged in a lengthy tirade against the pressure of social duties and unproductive drudgery that his high position involved. "If they would only let me alone!" he said; "I think it very hard that in the evening of my days I cannot order my life to suit my tastes. I have served the public long enough.... I would read—how I would read—and when I was bored I would sleep in my chair."

Success
"And yet," my friend said, commenting on these unguarded statements, "I believe he is the only person of his intimate circle who does not know that he would be hopelessly bored—that the things he decries are the very breath of life to him. There is absolutely no reason why he should not at once and forever realise his fancied ideal—and if his wife and children do not urge him to do so, it is only because they know that he would be absolutely miserable." And this is true of many lives.

If the "recognition," of which I have spoken above, were only accorded to the really eminent, it would be a somewhat different matter; but nine-tenths of the persons who receive it are nothing more than phantoms, who have set themselves to pursue the glory, without the services that ought to earn it. A great many people have a strong taste for power without work, for dignity without responsibility; and it is quite possible to attain consideration if you set yourself resolutely to pursue it.

The temptation comes in a yet more subtle form to men of a really high-minded type, whose chief preoccupation is earnest work and the secluded pursuit of some high ideal. Such people, though they do not wish to fetter themselves with the empty social duties that assail the eminent, yet are tempted to wish to have the refusal of them, and to be secretly dissatisfied if they do not receive this testimonial to the value of their work. The temptation is not so vulgar as it seems. Every one who is ambitious wishes to be effective. A man does not write books or paint pictures or make speeches simply to amuse himself, to fill his time; and they are few who can genuinely write, as the late Mark Pattison wrote of a period of his life, that his ideal was at one time "defiled and polluted by literary ambition."

Nevertheless, if there is to be any real attempt to win the inner peace of the spirit, such ambition must be not sternly but serenely resisted. Not until a man can pass by the rewards of fame oculis irretortis—"nor cast one longing, lingering look behind"—is the victory won.

Pure Ambition
It may be urged, in my case, that the obscurity for which I crave was never likely to be denied me. True; but at the same time ambition in its pettiest and most childish forms has been and is a real temptation to me: the ambition to dominate and dazzle my immediate circle, to stimulate curiosity about myself, to be considered, if not a successful man, at least a man who might have succeeded if he had cared to try—all the temptations which are depicted in so masterly and merciless a way by that acute psychologist Mr. Henry James in the character of Gilbert Osmond in the Portrait of a Lady—to all of these I plead guilty. Had I not been gifted with sufficient sensitiveness to see how singularly offensive and pitiful such pretences are in the case of others, I doubt if I should not have succumbed—if indeed I have not somewhat succumbed—to them.

Indeed, to some morbid natures such pretences are vital—nay, self-respect would be impossible without them. I know a lady who, like Mrs. Wittiterly, is really kept alive by the excitement of being an invalid. If she had not been so ill she would have died years ago. I know a worthy gentleman who lives in London and spends his time in hurrying from house to house lamenting how little time he can get to do what he really enjoys—to read or think. Another has come to my mind who lives in a charming house in the country, and by dint of inviting a few second-rate literary and artistic people to his house and entertaining them royally, believes himself to be at the very centre of literary and artistic life, and essential to its continuance. These are harmless lives, not unhappy, not useless; based, it is true, upon a false conception of the relative importance of their own existence, but then is there one of us—the most hard-working, influential, useful person in the world—who does not exaggerate his own importance? Does any one realise how little essential he is, or how easily his post is filled—indeed, how many people there are who believe that they could do the same thing better if they only had the chance.

A life to be happy must be compounded in due degree of activity and pleasure, using the word in its best sense. There must be sufficient activity to take off the perilous and acrid humours of the mind which, left to themselves, poison the sources of life, and enough pleasure to make the prospect of life palatable.

The first necessity is to get rid, as life goes on, of all conventional pleasures. By the age of forty a man should know what he enjoys, and not continue doing things intended to be pleasurable, either because he deludes himself into thinking that he enjoys them, or because he likes others to think that he enjoys them. I know now that I do not care for casual country-house visiting, for dancing, for garden parties, for cricket matches, and many another form of social distraction, but that the pleasures that remain and grow are the pleasures derived from books, from the sights and sounds of nature, from sympathetic conversation, from music, and from active physical exercise in the open air. It is my belief that a man is happiest who is so far employed that he has to scheme to secure a certain share of such pleasures. My own life unhappily is so ordered that it is the other way—that I have to scheme to secure sufficient activities to make such pleasure wholesome. But I am stern with myself. At times when I find the zest of simple home pleasures deserting me, I have sufficient self-control deliberately to spend a week in London, which I detest, or to pay a duty-visit where I am so acutely and sharply bored by a dull society—castigatio mea matutina est—that I return with delicious enthusiasm to my own trivial round.

Our Own Importance

I do not flatter myself that I hold any very important place in the world's economy. But I believe that I have humbly contributed somewhat to the happiness of others, and I find that the reward for thwarted, wasted ambitions has come in the shape of a daily increasing joy in quiet things and tender simplicities. I need not reiterate the fact that I draw from Nature, ever more and more, the most unfailing and the purest joy; and if I have forfeited some of the deepest and most thrilling emotions of the human heart, it is but what thousands are compelled to do; and it is something to find that the heart can be sweet and tranquil without them. The only worth of these pages must rest in the fact that the life which I have tried to depict is made up of elements which are within the reach of all or nearly all human beings. And though I cannot claim to have invented a religious system, or to have originated any new or startling theory of existence, yet I have proved by experiment that a life beset by many disadvantages, and deprived of most of the stimulus that to some would seem essential, need not drift into being discontented or evil or cold or hard.

33
Oct. 22, 1898.

That is, so to speak, the outside of my life, the front that is turned to the world. May I for a brief moment open the doors that lead to the secret rooms of the spirit?

The greater part of mankind trouble themselves little enough about the eternal questions: what we are, and what we shall be hereafter. Life to the strong, energetic, the full-blooded gives innumerable opportunities of forgetting. It is easy to swim with the stream, to take no thought of the hills which feed the quiet source of it, or the sea to which it runs; for such as these it is enough to live. But all whose minds are restless, whose imagination is constructive, who have to face some dreary and aching present, and would so gladly take refuge in the future and nestle in the arms of faith, if they could but find her—for these the obstinate question must come. Like the wind of heaven it rises. We may shut it out, trim the lamp, pile the fire, and lose ourselves in pleasant and complacent activities; but in the intervals of our work, when we drop the book or lay down the pen, the gust rises shrill and sharp round the eaves, the gale buffets in the chimney, and we cannot drown the echo in our hearts.

This is the question:—

Is our life a mere fortuitous and evanescent thing? Is consciousness a mere symptom of matter under certain conditions? Do we begin and end? Are the intense emotions and attachments, the joys and sorrows of life, the agonies of loss, the hungering love with which we surround the faces, the voices, the forms of those we love, the chords which vibrate in us at the thought of vanished days, and places we have loved—the old house, the family groups assembled, the light upon the quiet fields at evening, the red sunset behind the elms—all those purest, sweetest, most poignant memories—are these all unsubstantial phenomena like the rainbow or the dawn, subjective, transitory, moving as the wayfarer moves?

Who can tell us?

Some would cast themselves upon the Gospel—but to me it seems that Jesus spoke of these things rarely, dimly, in parables—and that though He takes for granted the continuity of existence, He deliberately withheld the knowledge of the conditions under which it continues. He spoke, it is true, in the story of Dives and Lazarus, of a future state, of the bosom of Abraham where the spirit rested like a tired child upon his father's knee—of the great gulf that could not be crossed except by the voices and gestures of the spirits—but will any one maintain that He was not using the forms of current allegory, and that He intended this parable as an eschatological solution? Again He spoke of the final judgment in a pastoral image.

Identity
Enough, some faithful souls may say, upon which to rest the hope of the preservation of human identity. Alas! I must confess with a sigh, it is not enough for me. I see the mass of His teaching directed to life, and the issues of the moment; I seem to see Him turn His back again and again on the future, and wave His followers away. Is it conceivable that if He could have said, in words unmistakable and precise, "You have before you, when the weary body closes its eyes on the world, an existence in which perception is as strong or stronger, identity as clearly defined, memory as real, though as swift as when you lived—and this too unaccompanied by any of the languors or failures or traitorous inheritance of the poor corporal frame,"— is it conceivable, I say, that if He could have said this, He would have held His peace, and spoken only through dark hints, dim allegories, shadowy imaginings. Could a message of peace more strong, more vital, more tremendous have been given to the world? To have satisfied the riddles of the sages, the dream of philosophers, the hopes of the ardent—to have allayed the fears of the timid the heaviness of the despairing; to have dried the mourner's tears—all in a moment. And He did not!

What then can we believe? I can answer but for myself.

I believe with my whole heart and soul in the indestructibility of life and spirit. Even matter to my mind seems indestructible—and matter is, I hold, less real than the motions and activities of the spirit.

It has sometimes seemed to me that matter may afford us the missing analogy: when the body dies, it sinks softly and resistlessly into the earth, and is carried on the wings of the wind, in the silent speeding fountains, to rise again in ceaseless interchange of form.

Individuality
Could it be so with life and spirit? As the fountain casts the jet high into the air over the glimmering basin, and the drops separate themselves for a prismatic instant—when their separate identity seems unquestioned—and then rejoin the parent wave, could not life and spirit slip back as it were into some vast reservoir of life, perhaps to linger there awhile, to lose by peaceful self-surrender, happy intermingling, by cool and tranquil fusion the dust, the

stain, the ghastly taint of suffering and sin? I know not, but I think it may be so.

But if I could affirm the other—that the spirit passes onwards through realms undreamed of, in gentle unstained communion, not only with those whom one has loved, but with all whom one ever would have loved, lost in sweet wonder at the infinite tenderness and graciousness of God—would it not in one single instant give me the peace I cannot find, and make life into a radiant antechamber leading to a vision of rapturous delight?

34
Sep. 18, 1900.

How can I write what has befallen me? the double disaster that has cut like a knife into my life. Was one, I asked myself, the result of the other, sent to me to show that I ought to have been content with what I had, that I ought not to have stretched out my hand to the fruit that hung too high above me. I am too feeble in mind and body to do more than briefly record the incidents that have struck me down. I feel like a shipwrecked sailor who, flung on an unhospitable shore, had with infinite labour and desperate toil dragged a few necessaries out of the floating fragments of the wreck, and piled them carefully and patiently on a ledge out of the reach of the tide, only to find after a night of sudden storm the little store scattered and himself swimming faintly in a raging sea—that sea which the evening before had sunk into so sweet, so caressing a repose, and now like a grey monster aroused to sudden fury, howls and beats for leagues against the stony promontories and the barren beaches.

New Friends

I had been in very tranquil spirits and strong health all the summer; my maladies had ceased to trouble me, and for weeks they were out of my thoughts. I had found a quiet zest in the little duties that make up my simple life. I had made, too, a new friend. A pleasant cottage about half a mile from Golden End had been taken by the widow of a clergyman with small but sufficient means, who settled there with her daughter, the latter being about twenty-four. I went somewhat reluctantly with my mother to call upon them and offer neighbourly assistance. I found myself at once in the presence of two refined, cultivated, congenial people. Mrs. Waring, I saw, was not only a well-read woman, interested in books and art, but she had seen something of society, and had a shrewd and humorous view of men and things. Miss Waring was like her mother; but I soon found that to her mother's kindly and brisk intellect she added a peculiar and noble insight—that critical power, if I may call it so, which sees what is beautiful and true in life, and strips it of adventitious and superficial disguises in the same way that one with a high appreciation of literature moves instinctively to what is gracious and lofty, and is never misled by talent or unobservant of genius. The society of these two became to me in a few weeks a real and precious possession. I began to see how limited and self-centred my life had begun to be. They did not, so to speak, provide me with new sensations and new material so much as put the whole of life in a new light. I found in the mother a wise and practical counsellor, with a singular grasp of detail, with whom I could discuss any new book I had read or any article that had struck me; but with Miss Waring it was different. I can only say that her wise and simple heart cast a new light upon the most familiar thoughts. I found myself understood, helped, lifted, in a way that both humiliated and inspired me. Moreover, I was privileged to be admitted into near relations with one who seemed to show, without the least consciousness of it, the best and highest possibilities that lie in human nature. I cannot guess or define the secret. I only know that it dawned upon me gradually that here was a human spirit fed like a spring from the purest rains that fall on some purple mountain-head.

The Moment
By what soft and unsuspected degrees my feeling of congenial friendship grew into a deeper devotion I cannot now trace. It must now in my miserable loneliness be enough to say that so it was. Only a few days ago—and yet the day seems already to belong to a remote past, and to be separated from these last dark hours by a great gulf, misty, not to be passed,—I realised that a new power had come into my life—the heavenly power that makes all things new. I had gone down to the cottage in a hot, breathless sunlight afternoon. I had long passed the formality of ringing to announce my entrance. There was no one in the little drawing-room, which was cool and dark, with shuttered windows. I went out upon the lawn. Miss Waring was sitting in a chair under a beech tree reading, and at the sight of me she rose, laid down her book, and came smiling across the grass. There is a subtle, viewless message of the spirit which flashes between kindred souls, in front of and beyond the power of look or speech, and at the same moment that I understood I felt she understood too. I could not then at once put into words my hopes; but it hardly seemed necessary. We sat together, we spoke a little, but were mostly silent in some secret interchange of spirit. That afternoon my heart climbed, as it were, a great height, and saw from a Pisgah top the familiar land at its feet, all lit with a holy radiance, and then turning, saw, in golden gleams and purple haze, the margins of an unknown sea stretching out beyond the sunset to the very limits of the world.

35
Sep. 19, 1900.

That night, in a kind of rapturous peace, I faced the new hope. Even then, in that august hour, I reflected whether I could, with my broken life and faded dreams, link a spirit so fair to mine. I can truthfully say that I was full to the brim of the intensest gratitude, the tenderest service; but I thought was it just, was it right, with little or nothing to offer, to seek to make so large a claim upon so beautiful a soul? I did not doubt that I could win it, and that love would be lavished in fullest measure to me. But I strove with all my might to see whether such a hope was not on my part a piece of supreme and shameful selfishness. I probed the very depths of my being, and decided that I might dare; that God had given me this precious, this adorable gift, and that I might consecrate my life and heart to love and be worthy of it if I could.

So I sank to sleep, and woke to the shock of a rapture such as I did not believe this world could hold. It was a still warm day of late summer, but a diviner radiance lay over garden, field, and wood for me. I determined I would not speak to my mother till after I had received my answer.

After breakfast I went out to the garden—the flowers seemed to smile and nod their heads at me, leaning with a kind of tender brilliance to greet me; in a thick bush I heard the flute-notes of my favourite thrush—the brisk chirruping of the sparrows came from the ivied gable.

What was it?... what was the strange, rending, numbing shock that ran so suddenly through me, making me in a moment doubtful, as it seemed, even of my own identity—again it came—again. I raised my eyes, it seemed as if I had never seen the garden, the house, the trees before. Then came a pang of such grim horror that I felt as though stabbed with a sword. I seemed, if that is possible, almost to smell and taste pain. I staggered a few steps back to the garden entrance—I remember crying out faintly, and my voice seemed strange to me—there was a face at the door—and then a blackness closed round me and I knew no more.

36
Sep. 20, 1900.

I woke at last, swimming upwards, like a diver out of a deep sea, from some dark abyss of weakness. I opened my eyes—I saw that I was in a downstairs room, where it seemed that a bed must have been improvised; but at first I was too weak even to inquire with myself what had happened. My mother sate by me, with a look on her face that I had never seen; but I could not care. I seemed to have passed a ford, and to see life from the other side; to have shut a door upon it, and to be looking at it from the dark window. I neither cared nor hoped nor felt. I only wished to lie undisturbed—not to be spoken to or noticed, only to lie.

I revived a little, and the faint flow of life brought back with it, as upon a creeping tide, a regret that I had opened my eyes upon the world again—that was my first thought. I had been so near the dark passage—the one terrible thing that lies in front of all living things—why had I not been permitted to cross it once and for all; why was I recalled to hope, to suffering, to fear? Then, as I grew stronger, came a fuller regret for the good, peaceful days. I had asked, I thought, so little of life, and that little had been denied. Then as I grew stronger still, there came the thought of the great treasure that had been within my grasp, and my spirit faintly cried out against the fierce injustice of the doom. But I soon fell into a kind of dimness of thought, from which even now I can hardly extricate myself—a numbness of heart, an indifference to all but the fact that from moment to moment I am free from pain.

37
Sep. 21, 1900.

I am climbing, climbing, hour by hour, slowly and cautiously, out of the darkness, as a man climbs up some dizzy crag, never turning his head—yet not back to life! I shall not achieve that.

How strange it would seem to others that I can care to write thus—it seems strange even to myself. If ever, in life, I looked on to these twilight hours, with the end coming slowly nearer, I thought I should lie in a kind of stupor of mind and body, indifferent to everything. I am indifferent, with the indifference of one in whom desire seems to be dead; but my mind is, or seems, almost preternaturally clear; and the old habit, of trying to analyse, to describe, anything that I see or realise distinctly is too strong for me. I have asked for pencil and paper; they demur, but yield; and so I write a little, which relieves the occasional physical restlessness I feel; it induces a power of tranquil reverie, and the hours pass, I hardly know how. The light changes; the morning freshness becomes the grave and solid afternoon, and so dies into twilight; till out of the dark alleys steals the gentle evening, dark-eyed and with the evening star tangled in her hair, full of shy sweet virginal thoughts and mysteries ... and then the night, and the day again.

Do I grieve, do I repine, do I fear? No, I can truthfully say, I do not. I hardly seem to feel. Almost the only feeling left me is the old childlike trustfulness in mother and nurse. I do not seem to need to tell them anything. One or other sits near me. I feel my mother's eyes dwell upon me, till I look up and smile; but between our very minds there runs, as it were, an airy bridge, on which the swift thoughts, the messengers of love, speed to and fro. I seem, in the loss of all the superstructure and fabric of life, to have nothing left to tie me to the world, but this sense of unity with my mother—that inseparable, elemental tie that nothing can break. And she, I know, feels this too; and it gives her, though she could not describe it, a strange elation in the midst of her sorrow, the joy that a man is born into the world, and that I am hers.

A Mother's Heart

With the beloved nurse it is the same in a sense; but here it is not the deep inextricable bond of blood, but the bond of perfect love. I lose myself in wonder in thinking of it; that one who is hired—that is the strange basis of the relationship—for a simple task, should become absolutely identified with love, with those whom she serves. I do not believe that Susan has a single thought or desire in the world that is not centred on my mother or myself. The tie between us is simply indissoluble. And I feel that if we wandered, we three spirits, disconsolate and separate, through the trackless solitudes of heaven, she would somehow find her way to my side.

I have noticed that since my illness began she has slipped into the use of little nursery phrases which I have not heard for years; I have become "Master Henry" again, and am told to "look slippy" about taking my medicine. This would have moved me in other days with a sense of pathos; it is not so now, though the knowledge that these two beloved, sweet-minded, loving women suffer, is the one shadow over my tranquillity. If I could only explain to them that my sadness for their sorrow is drowned in my wonder at the strangeness that any one should ever sorrow at all for anything!

38
Sep. 22, 1900.

To-day I am calmer, and the hours have been passing in a long reverie; I have been thinking quietly over the past years. Sometimes, as I lay with eyes closed, the old life came so near me that it almost seemed as if men and women and children, some of them dead and gone, had sate by me and spoken to me; little scenes and groups out of early years that I thought I had forgotten suddenly shaped themselves. It is as if my will had abdicated its sway, and the mind, like one who is to remove from a house in which he had long dwelt, is turning over old stores, finding old relics long laid aside in cupboards and lumber-rooms, and seeing them without sorrow, only lingering with a kind of tender remoteness over the sweet and fragrant associations of the days that are dead.

I have never doubted that I am to die, and to-day it seems as though I cared little when the parting comes; death does not seem to me now like a sharp close to life, the yawning of a dark pit; but, as in an allegory, I seem to see a little dim figure, leaving a valley full of sunlight and life, and going upwards into misty and shapeless hills. I used to wonder whether death was an end, an extinction—now that seems impossible—my life and thought seem so strong, so independent of the frail physical accompaniments of the body; but even if it is an end, the thought does not afflict me. I am in the Father's hands. It is He that hath made us.

39
Sep. 24, 1900.

I have had an interview with her. I hardly know what we said—very little—she understood, and it was very peaceful in her presence. I tried to tell her not to be sorry; for indeed the one thing that seems to me inconceivable is that any one should grieve. I lie like a boat upon a quiet tide, drifting out to sea—the sea to which we must all drift. I am thankful for my life and all its sweetness; the shadows have gone, and it seems to me now as though all the happiness came from God, and all the shadow was of my own making. And the strangest thought of all is that the darkest shadow has always been this very passing which now seems to me the most natural thing in the world—indeed the only true thing.

None the less am I thankful for this great and crowning gift of love—the one thing that I had missed. I do not now even want to use it, to enjoy it—it is there, and that is enough. In her presence it seemed to me that Love stood side by side with Death, two shining sisters. But yesterday I murmured over having been given, as it were, so sweet a cup to taste, and then having the cup dashed from my lips. To-day I see that Love was the crown of my poor life, and I thank God with all the strength of my spirit for putting it into my hand as His last and best gift.

And I thanked her too for deigning to love me; and even while I did so, the thought broke to pieces, as it were, and escaped from the feeble words in which I veiled it, like a moth bursting from a cocoon. For were we not each other's before the world was made? And the thought of myself and herself fled from me, and we were one spirit, thinking the same thoughts, sustained by the same strength. One more word I said, and bade her believe that I said it with undimmed and unblunted mind, that she must live, and cast abroad by handfuls the love she would have garnered for me; that the sorrow that lay heavy on her heart must be fruitful, not a devastating sorrow; and that however much alone she might seem, that I should be there, like one who kneels without a closed door ... and so we said farewell.

Nearly Home
I lie now in my own room—it is evening; through the open window I can see the dark-stemmed trees, the pigeon-cotes, the shadowy shoulder of the barn, the soft ridges beyond, the little wood-end that I saw once in the early dawn and thought so beautiful. When I saw it before it seemed to me like the gate of the unknown country; will my hovering spirit pass that way? I have lived my little life—and my heart goes out to all of every tribe and nation under the sun who are still in the body. I would tell them with my last breath that there is comfort to the end—that there is nothing worth fretting over or being heavy-hearted about it; that the Father's arm is strong, and that his Heart is very wide.

THE END.

Printed in Great Britain
by Amazon